THE DESERT REMAINS

The Desert Remains

Charles C. Poling

UNIVERSITY OF NEW MEXICO PRESS ■ ALBUQUERQUE

© 2007 by Charles C. Poling
All rights reserved. Published 2007
Printed in the United States of America
13   12   11   10   09   08   07   1   2   3   4   5   6   7

    Library of Congress Cataloging-in-Publication Data
    Poling, Charles.
    The desert remains / Charles C. Poling.
       p. cm.
    ISBN 978-0-8263-4257-7 (cloth : alk. paper)
    1. Ranches—New Mexico—Fiction.
    2. New Mexico—Fiction.
    3. Domestic fiction.
    I. Title.
    PS3616.O5674D47 2007
    813'.6—dc22
    2007009523

Design and composition: Melissa Tandysh

All people, places, and events
in this account are fictitious.

■

Acknowledgments

A few key people nudged, encouraged, and corrected my course as a novelist. Thanks for that go to Lon Holmberg, who probably saw more ambition in me than talent thirty years ago; to Patricia Hummer, a penetrating reader of an early draft of this novel; and to Tony Hillerman, that paragon of commitment to the craft of writing and a mentor for the ages. Most of all, I am indebted to my wife, Mary Boliek, for her unflinching insight into these characters, without which I would not have solved the crux problem of the novel.

1.

DANIEL IS LATE FOR THE FUNERAL, but when he spots the horse herd near the highway he pulls over and gets out of the car. Standing still, he inhales the sharp desert air, then lets it out, and in the space between he finds everything and nothing. That is enough for this moment, but it will not last. Ruby will see to that.

He walks to the edge of an escarpment where the highway drops into a small canyon, then rises in a broad curve across the flats by the abandoned Willard ranch. In the cold wind his eyes well up, streaming thick tears across his cheekbones, but he is not crying. His flawed grief is crowded aside by a more urgent compulsion both thrilling and tainted, yet all the while this landscape tugs at him gently, patiently courting his attention. Beyond the flats below him, the ranch cliffs plow through slow-drifting, dense white snow squalls, lit obliquely by sunlight lancing from heavy clouds farther west. Storm obliterates the river canyon. To Daniel's left, Las Animas Peak stands headless under the low cloud ceiling.

He remembers hiking a mesa ridgeline over there in high summer and finding a skeletal deer's leg, joints still intact, hoof intact too. He could flex it at the knee. It had thrilled him like some talisman slipped into his hand from behind in a large crowd, though he had not looked back over his shoulder to see—who?—and of course he had been alone.

He had hung the leg by its crook over the branch of a piñon tree and continued his walk, wondering what predator's eyes traced his shadow slipping like dark water across the brilliant desert. On his way back he had hunted for that tree but never could find it again: the desert confounded his sense of direction and swallowed it up. If he had been riding Turk, he might have found the way. His horse could often retrace his own tracks months or even a year later. Daniel lacks such infallible homing instincts except toward Ruby: he is heading for her now.

Time enough for that. He calls to his horse—"Turk!"—cupping his hands to his mouth and hollering into the wind: "Turrrrk!" almost yodeling. The animals ignore him or perhaps they are too far away to hear. Some graze intently, while a few—including his gelding—stand with rumps to the wind and heads hung down, half asleep. In this turbulent cold autumn weather, Daniel wishes Turk were in the corral where someone could keep an eye on him. The gelding loses weight on pasture and often strays far from the herd. Daniel imagines that one day he will return to the ranch and the horse will be gone, wandered off into the mesas and canyons to the north, leaving Daniel with one less excuse to come here in Ruby's absence. He has no idea what he would do without this place.

He drives up the ranch road. The forked crest of Mesa Reina rises like outstretched, embracing arms, folding him into the heart of Rancho de Las Animas. The cliffs are vivid red and orange and yellow. Between the wings of Mesa Reina and directly in his line of travel he can see the dark cut of Water Canyon and the cottonwoods around the ranch buildings, still a mile off. The rutted road drops off a grassy rise and crosses the arroyo where his friend and sometime cowboying partner, Lester, has with perfect care fitted a stone retaining wall to keep the stream from cutting away the roadbed after every hard rain.

A bit farther along, Daniel slows for the big curve along the bottom of the alfalfa field. He has spent countless hours on the tractor here, plowing and seeding and mowing hay or pulling the huge field sprinklers to the next dry spot on this sloping patch of farmland. He keeps the car purring along in second gear past the fields. Ahead he can see the gathering of cars and trucks nosed-in around the chapel that was built in Spanish colonial days, fell into decay, then was resurrected by Tomás Lucero in the 1960s and the Penitente brothers at the urging of Rae McCullough, the owner of the ranch, and to the dismay and confusion of her husband, Calvin. Now, in October 1978, it will host Rae's funeral.

Returning to the ranch seems to collapse all time, just as the distance from Ruby will soon foreshorten in the coming back and nothing that has happened in the meantime, no place they have gone from each other, has any bearing on this continuous present rooted in their shared history. Here in this eternal place everything will unfold, or has unfolded and awaits only his awakening. Thus has the ranch always been—the potential for sudden insight—and she his guide, she his master. Only here has he found no loneliness that is not solitude, no loss that is not opportunity, no desire that is not patience. Back again, he discovers the place has never left him but instead has lodged under his skin, awaiting release in one instant of resolution and final transformation.

Daniel reaches the chapel and parks the car on the grass

off to the side. With a slight nervous trembling he heads for the entry, joining the loose line of friends, acquaintances, and familiar faces he has waved to for a few years now, when they passed on the highway—men in bolo ties and newly polished black cowboy boots, women who have pinned their long hair back with beaded barrettes, some wearing crisp new Levi's, others in more formal attire, closet-weary dresses of navy blue, forest green, or even black. By his friends he is greeted like a returning son, his hand shaken, his arms coaxed into a clutching hug. Ruby is nowhere in sight.

Finally Daniel faces Ruby's father. Wiry and square shouldered, mild mannered, calm even now, Calvin reaches out to clasp hands, his body nearly exhausted of movement, his face stilled and sagging from fatigue, his thinning red hair not combed so much as pressed downward against his head by a hat. Yet he manages a smile. "I'm glad you could come, Dan."

"I had to, Calvin. I just had to," Daniel answers, wondering how these recent events will further skew his already off-center orbit around this eccentric family.

"Well, thank you—" and their hands remain tightly gripped, the words they exchange subordinate to the years of friendship and other complexities expressed by that touch.

Daniel searches the room for Ruby as the minister approaches, rests his hands on Calvin's shoulders from behind, and gently ushers him away, saying, "It's time to start, Cal." Daniel will have to connect with Ruby later. The two older men move to the front of the chapel, which is filled with a flat gray light that casts no shadows. Deep, vertical windows to the east draw the eye to the sandstone cliffs, their livid bands of color uncharacteristically muted by the dim day. High above the stubbled alfalfa field, a raven and magpie duel, the magpie darting at the bigger bird and wheeling away. A few

snowflakes fly, light and buoyant in the wind, some even fluttering upward.

Daniel greets Lester with a prolonged handshake and a
quiet "howdy." Lester is bereft too, but he occupies a peculiar
intersection in the web of survivors. He and Daniel will talk
later. Daniel takes a seat beside him on a metal chair near the
back like a spectator at a passion play, like always.

People are still filing in, the Trujillos and Scotts and
Martinezes, gathering along the back wall, standing in small
groups. Then from the side door Ruby enters, medievally
cloaked in a wool overcoat that drapes over her shoulders like
a cape, her arms not in the sleeves, her rich dark hair falling
like a hood about her face. Daniel registers her appearance
with a heightened pulse, hopes to catch her eye, to make some
meaningful gesture of sympathy across the distance, but her
attention is riveted to the floor. With her brother, Harvey, she
glides to the first pew and sits, a tissue crumpled into a ball in
her hand, now pressed to her nose.

The minister opens with a prayer that Daniel can't follow.
Instead he watches Calvin standing by the podium with his
head piously bent. Daniel thinks of the disturbing dream of
fire he had the night Rae died. It has assumed an uncanny pre-
science since he learned how the Turkey Springs house—her
personal retreat on the ranch, a hermitage away from marriage
and family—burned down around her. He remembers Rae's
otherly strangeness and wonders if Calvin had been showered
with the fallout of his wife's death in a dream, or a spurious
memory, or a vague burning sensation.

Calvin had taken Harvey over to Mosquero to buy cattle,
and of course Ruby was living in California. Perhaps Rae had
not wanted her family around, he thinks. Perhaps fire was the
only way she could die, a foreordained consummation of her

life, neither precisely intentional nor accidental but always imminent. Brooding, weird, never quite happy and more usually cross, Rae had lived with the wariness of the once-defeated who mistrusts present good fortune. She was prone to silence and depression, often keeping the living room curtains drawn at midday, the room dark and indistinct against the piercing sunlit clarity of the desert beyond the glass. It was an open secret that she and Calvin had not lived together as man and wife for many years. They conspired in darker secrets too, mysteries that Daniel has yet to penetrate.

Calvin will speak now. He steps to the lectern, his large, blunt fingers fumbling with reading glasses, which age him dramatically, then shuffling through the index cards, no doubt a set of carefully ordered notes. Daniel remembers Calvin had attended a Presbyterian seminary before heading off to Alaska for missionary work in Sitka, then returning to marry Rae and help her run her family's ranch.

A magpie, perhaps the one battling the raven above the field minutes ago, chatters from a branch of the old cottonwood that shades the chapel in summertime, chatters to no one in particular above the strained quiet of those gathered to mourn as they clear their throats and shuffle their feet on the linoleum floor. Rae would have been impatient, Daniel thinks. In her faint nasal drawl she would have hurried Calvin through the eulogy while her calloused hands kept busy in back, setting out plastic foam cups and packets of coffee creamer.

A light ringing sound like silver bells fills the chapel: Ruby is crying. As softly as rain on aspen leaves, as quiet as melting snow, she weeps. Everyone listens, noiseless and motionless, except Calvin. He considers Ruby over the top of his glasses, his face bland and remote. He finds voice to recite the details of Rae's childhood, their meeting and subsequent marriage in

Alaska—the facts of an obituary, as dry as newsprint. Then he pauses, takes off his glasses, tucks the index cards into his suit's inner pocket, and says, "This morning, I told Harvey and Maryanne"—for that is Ruby's given name—"that life for their mother had always been more difficult than most. Yet she trusted in God to ease her path, to light the way. And last Sunday that light failed." The final word is squeezed and deformed as Calvin gulps, his eyes snapping between Ruby and Harv; he even smiles, and Ruby's face is now turned up toward her father, her torso cocked at an angle to him defensively, while Daniel senses a specific but unspoken communication pass through the stricken family, a confession or admission, and a petition for forgiveness. Daniel must look away to the windows.

The magpie is gone.

After a hymn and closing prayer, Tomás Lucero takes charge. He stands beside the minister and announces that burial will be performed by the Penitente Brothers immediately, below the cliffs of Capilla Peak. Daniel and Lester stay seated as the others clot through the door.

"Did you know you're a pallbearer?" Lester asks.

"No!" Daniel replies, an anxious rippling in his gut. "I wouldn't have been late. Are you too?"

"Hell, yeah!"

Tomás stands near the head of the casket, speaking softly to Calvin.

Lester nods toward them and says, "They're probably trying to figure out how wide the hole should be," and they both smile not because it is a joke, but because it is probably true: the men are discussing the grave as they would talk over installing a cattle guard, not heartless but ever practical. In work they find release from grief and more shadowy, unsanctioned emotions. "Calvin was out at six thirty digging with the back hoe."

The other pallbearers have gathered at the front, and the seats around Daniel are empty. Ruby and Harvey have not moved, each preoccupied by internal visions, or the simple blankness of grief. To further postpone greeting Ruby, Daniel turns to Lester and says very quietly, "How did the fire start?"

"Uh, well, about that—"

With six men lifting, the casket is surprisingly light as they slide it into the back end of Calvin's rusty International Scout. Tomás guides the activities with respectful dignity. Ruby has gone ahead to the pickup truck driven by her brother. As the group disperses, Daniel feels a hand squeeze his arm above the elbow, turns to find Calvin. Eyes swollen, he points toward the Scout with pursed lips, a habitual gesture Daniel has seen a thousand times. "Will you two drive it up?" the older man asks, the word *it* hanging between them, each aware how the semantic change from *her* has diminished their lives, and Daniel feels the hand tighten on his arm as Calvin steadies himself. "Anyway, someone needs to drive. I need to drive Ruby and Harvey and we don't all fit in the Scout, not in Ruby's good clothes. I don't know why they loaded it in the Scout anyhow."

"I'll drive," Daniel offers.

Lester already is climbing into the passenger seat. Calvin strides away in his bowlegged, rolling gait. Daniel checks that the Scout is in four-wheel drive, then eases it forward into the muddy ruts, driving alongside the alfalfa field, then dipping down where the road follows the creek.

"How are you doing?" he asks.

Lester manages to shrug with only his eyebrows and his lower lip.

"How's Ruby taking it?"

"About like you'd expect, I guess," Lester says. "She'll make it."

"I hope so."

"Well, it's going to get ugly for a while. That girl's loaded for bear," Lester says.

"I guess," Daniel says, though he knows far less than Lester does about the McCullough family's emotional currents and eddies, caught up in them though he may be. "What do you mean?"

"Ruby's got a lot to sort out. Let's leave it at that." Lester looks away, out the side window. "She was worried you wouldn't come."

"Of course I came."

"I don't think there's anyone else she can really talk to," Lester suggests.

The Scout veers almost sideways as the road crosses a small tributary arroyo, all greasy wet clay, and Lester twists around to check the casket. "I'd hate to drop that thing out the back." Daniel looks sideways at him, then they both laugh, high and giddy. "Jesus."

"God, it seemed so light," Daniel says. Lester is watching him closely, a slight, expectant smile further creasing his Viking features. "What aren't you telling me?" Daniel asks him.

"She's not in it."

"What?"

"Calvin drove her into the mesas somewhere—way back in—somewhere on Mesa Reina, I think. No one is supposed to know. I helped him load her into the truck. Not buried or anything. Indian style. He was gone a good long time. She told him once that's how she wanted it to be. Out there with the birds and coyotes. Dust to dust, you know?"

Daniel has stopped the truck, an enormous lump in his throat. Together they sit still as the sun breaks through to shine on the brown-leaved oaks that line the arroyo and the taller trees too. He imagines her corpse propped against an ancient piñon tree or reclining skyward atop an elevated rack of aspens high on the rocky point of Mesa Reina where the wind never stops blowing and the valley gapes away as vast as memory but more distinct, where the crumbled wall of a thousand-year-old pueblo accelerates the backward plunge of rock slabs and floury soil and time itself, where ravens gather carrion like wisdom, then scatter to the four winds, where nothing is spoken, and the world reclaims—

Then it starts to snow, fat flakes swirling in a gusting wind, the sun washing this squall pale yellow as people walk by the stationary truck, their heads bent to the wet snow, moving like ghosts as the wind blasts harder, a whiteout erasing the trees ten feet away, but still the mourners move by, appearing from the backlit cloud with heads bent, their movements restrained and bizarrely abstract against the gauzy background. Then they fade into the storm as they climb the hill from the arroyo toward the burial site: they rise upward into the cloud. Daniel sits spellbound. The squall blasts even harder, like a wild thing, shaking the Scout, whistling at the windows trying to get inside. The muddy ground whitens.

2.

AT THE GRAVE, Ruby shines from within, aglow like the sun now slanting across the white desert to etch with vivid shadow every juniper sprig and clump of sagebrush, so that Daniel as he climbs from the Scout feels possessed of preternatural vision. He walks toward her, and though she stands beside Harvey with her head bent, he can sense her waiting and her concentration on his approach, not coy, but patient, and when she rises into his arms to embrace him, she says, "My mother was freakin' crazy," in a jagged angry voice, "but I can't believe she killed herself."

"I'm so sorry," Daniel says. "Just tell me how I can help." He holds her and she squeezes him so tight his backbone pops, a muffled crunching that brings her face up in surprise to regard him, her brown eyes afloat in tears, a startled smile unwrapping her white teeth, and Daniel smiles too at the incongruity and pleasure of such a small joke. Then Harvey steps forward to shake his hand, and Ruby backs off, her hand hesitantly sliding from his arm as if to prolong touching, her head bowing slightly in embarrassment and apparent confusion. Harvey's grip is damp, his already-fleshy face swollen and uncannily resembling Calvin's as the boy balances on the cusp of manhood. Daniel murmurs clichés of consolation.

Harvey moves off to help Tomás and the others haul the casket out of the Scout. They set a few two-by-fours on the ground to keep the wood clean of mud. The pile of exhumed dirt beside the grave is whitened like a snowdrift. Several boulders the size of boxcars frame the burial site, resting where they fell five or twenty or a thousand years ago, one day and without apparent provocation shearing away from the slab-sided mesa, its south face vertically fluted three hundred feet high as though chisel-carved, with angular facets rising up its full height. Daniel stands wordless beside Ruby and they watch the casket as the men place it beside the grave. People have gathered in a rough crescent around the south end of the hole, all watching.

"How do they put it down in?" he asks.

"With ropes. It'll be lowered," she says.

Hands still in his pockets, he asks, "Are you all right? Do you want to stay? I could take you back to the house."

"I'm all right," she says, and her voice is marble smooth now. She looks south toward the reservoir, the valley past it, and the peaks on the horizon. With the restless changeability of autumn, the clouds have cleared to the west, though still the wind blows, and the sun flows warmly across Daniel's face, glows and reddens on Ruby's dark cheeks and hair. Still looking away, she nods toward the pond almost as Calvin would nod and says, "Do you remember when we went swimming there that summer? Mom got pretty upset. She thought I'd catch a disease from the water."

She turns back to Daniel, her heavy lashes half lowered. "A social disease, I suppose. I must have been sixteen."

And beautiful, he thinks, leggy as a Thoroughbred, brown as clay, tantalizing as a Siren.

"I had more chance of catching something at home. . . . But I never skinny-dipped there with anyone else," she says, and he thinks, Why is she talking about all this now? As thin tears streak from her eyes, she straightens up, her face open to the wind and sun. Rippling waves shimmer across the pond like shining strands of silver *heishi*. Lester and Harvey are working around the coffin, sliding a heavy nylon strap under it, then another. Tomás moves to the head of the grave and Calvin walks toward his daughter and Daniel, stepping between them like a wedge. Already the thin snow melts from the slopes facing the sun.

"I'd better go help," Daniel says tentatively, feeling like an intruder, uncertain whether his affection for Ruby is trumped by Calvin's paternal authority.

The other pallbearers gather by the casket. Daniel awaits release by Ruby, whose eyes flutter toward him and then harden onto her father. After awkwardly patting Calvin's granite shoulder, Daniel steps past them and takes a place by Lester and Harvey, their backs to the wind, which rustles their pant legs like flags on a mast.

With a natural air of command suspending his own grief, Tomás raises his hand invokingly and holds it out from his body, shoulder high, gathering silence from the people, accumulating their attention. Daniel focuses on Ruby, who—restless and agitated as a filly in a storm—glances quickly around her as if measuring a threat, shuffling slightly away from Calvin, her father clasping his hands reverently before him like a good deacon, then she seems to gather herself. Her chest swells with a deep breath. She shakes her hair from her shoulders and tilts her face to the sky, the nervous motion of her body, the prancing horse energy pouring outward, upward, toward—

The gathered silence now pooling under Tomás's cupped hand, a gentle swirling eddy of human attention lapping the edges of the grave, Ruby's face still upturned—Daniel can't take his eyes off her. While Tomás intones a Penitente prayer, all other heads bowed, in sudden vertigo he feels he is looking up at her from far below and the rapid Spanish words swirl around him in arcing trails of sound like shooting stars, indecipherable portents, a revelatory message slipping by, rushing over him and by him and pulling at him too, a current of confusion pulling at him, sucking at him like a whirlpool, and still she stands like carved stone.

He sways and must take a step to steady himself, dips his head and puts his fingers to his eyes, sees only a black shroud of dizziness. The darkness passes, and when he looks up again Ruby's eyes await him. All other heads are bowed. Tomás has stopped speaking, the wind has paused, their heads are bowed, her awaiting eyes freeze him to the moment, command him to be still, to wait with her for—

Lester stepping by jostles him and when he looks back she is speaking to Calvin, her face set tight, her words garbled to his ears but not her emphatic tone. Calvin's expression sours. Daniel rouses himself and moves to the coffin, helps lift it by the ropes, and with Lester beside him backs toward and around the grave, so the casket is suspended over it. Slowly, with Tomás steadying the box, the men lower it to rest far down in the earth on the boards, then they slide the ropes from beneath it and the job is done. Lester looks at Daniel and there are no words. Daniel turns to see Calvin bear-hugging Harvey, who is crying in heavy, lunging gulps, Calvin patting his back, holding him up. Beside them Ruby stands desolate, a space seemingly cleared around her. She looks forward at nothing, her eyes vacant, her face formless as water.

Tomás stoops to the pile of dirt, grabs a handful, and tosses it into the grave, where it rattles onto the wood. He stands a moment, seemingly at a loss, as if his script had ended, then he walks to the Scout, slides a shovel out of the back end, and leans against it. Now Lester digs his fingers into the sticky mud, clenches it into a ball, and heaves it into the hole. He walks over to Tomás. They stand easily beside each other, the tall Viking and the compact *genizaro*, the backbone workers on this ranch, who each shared a part of Rae but Daniel can't pinpoint what it was. An intimacy that passed over his head, he thinks.

Others imitate their action, filing past one by one, some murmuring prayers or crossing themselves, and still Ruby has not moved until Calvin takes her by the arm and her body goes tight as he guides her toward his pickup, helps her onto the seat, then heads back toward the grave and the dirt pile.

Daniel forgoes the dirt ritual and heads for Ruby. She opens the door and he slides to the middle of the seat so he can sit beside her. In the close cab he is struck by her scent, a faintly sweet odor of flowers, a tropical air, a garden, even, where—

"I'm just putting up with him today and he knows it," Ruby says. Then her voice softens: "I felt her so strongly, just then," she says. "Did you? You did. She was right there with me. And you—" Her voice trails off, thin, girlish, wisping. Then: "Why was she so fucking weird? They both are. I feel cursed!" And a while later, after he has reached for her hand and gently held it like a fallen bird: "Thank you so much for being here." Again she cries softly and with patience, still sitting upright and watching the world beyond the window, where birds flutter among the trees and sagebrush quivers stiffly in the wind. "I'm going to flood the world away," she manages with a flickering smile. Then she leans away from him and locks his eyes. "But I want you to know, I'm not crying for her. Not for Dad, either. I'm crying for myself. That's the first thing you should know. Take me home."

"I'll tell your dad," he says, opening the door, but her hand catches him.

"No!"

He looks to the grave, where Lester and Tomás steadily shovel dirt into the hole. Calvin squats near them, alone, watching the work. Harvey sits behind the wheel of the Scout, one of his friends with him.

"They can all ride in Tomás's truck."

"Okay," Daniel agrees. He eases out the door and walks around the front of the truck as patches of sandstone blaze in the sunshine and tiny clouds of steam rise from the hillsides across the arroyo. He pauses and scans the flat ridgeline of Mesa Reina to the north, above the cliffs where the piñons give way to ponderosa pine and elk crash through underbrush and bound over the muddy streambeds, but he sees only the glistening rock and opaque blue sky and no clue to her final resting place.

They drive in silence, the truck sliding through the mud and bogging on the uphills. Daniel parks in the circular driveway where he has parked a hundred other times and she makes no move to get out. Below them the flats stretch barren toward the river, then again to the base of Las Animas, the forested face of the mountain scarred by a thin meadow of snow near its summit.

"Do you want me to come in?" he offers.

She nods and whispers, "Yes."

The house is dim and Ruby busies herself opening shades. Daniel stands in the living room, which is cluttered with unearthed and ancient artifacts—pots, scrapers, metates, clay fetishes—and he looks out the west-facing picture window. Once he had stood in this same spot and asked Rae's permission to escort Ruby to a New Year's dance in the gym at Los Ojos, and Rae had glared coldly, protectively at him for a moment before answering, while Calvin sat in the study with his reading glasses on and punched numbers on an adding machine.

He realizes that Ruby is quiet somewhere and finds her in the kitchen, leaning against a counter still wearing the long wool coat, hugging herself, calm and composed, looking at him clear-eyed and with hope.

"Are you cold? The house feels chilly," he says.

She shakes her head "no" but he goes to the hallway thermostat anyway and sets it to seventy, then returns.

"I wish it was summer," she says. "We could go for a walk." She falls quiet again, drops her eyes, and the silence and artificial light of the kitchen press in upon Daniel so that he feels miles underground and again dizzy, as though his senses are not to be trusted or he has suddenly and for the first time felt the rotation of the earth whipping him around through space, a disorientation visual and compressing, rendering suspicious all the relationships between objects he had once assumed without question.

He wavers slightly and again her eyes are upon him, steadying him, deep watery pools, as complicated and unfathomable as Sanskrit: he thinks of water, Ruby as sleek as an otter guiding him under into a warm darkness, a rhythmic darkness, a musical darkness, wriggling through an aperture of black rock intricately carved with geometrical and faceless people whose heads are spirals, their torsos diamonds, wriggling through ahead of him into another pool of Caribbean blue cut deeply by glittering columns of light, its surface far above brilliant and piercing as a carpet of sunlit crystals gently undulating and flashing reds, blues, greens, yellows. A rainbow of disintegrated white light, she glides upward through the glittering columns, glides upward through the light away from him trailing a shower of color like a full-spectrum comet, but the rock aperture blocks his pursuit and he can only shove his head through to watch her recede—

He wavers slightly and her eyes remain upon him, steadying him. "You should have made love to me that time," she replies.

"What?" His breath comes shallow.

"When we were swimming. In the water. I wanted you, I was ready. That's what you're thinking about, isn't it? My mother always said she'd castrate any boy who screwed me. It was a joke, she said. Like a commandment. But she meant it, of course," Ruby adds. "With certain specific exceptions."

On that day so hot he could smell the sandstone and the very blueness of the sky, he had stepped out of his hiking shorts and into the pond, its chill deflating his momentary arousal and she had ordered his eyes shut while she disrobed.

Standing chest deep he had heard a susurration like the wind in willows, then a weightier splashing and she swam past him with strong and precise strokes toward the middle of the pond, where she rolled twice, then faced him, treading water, smiling spectacularly. So erect it hurt, he sank deeper into the water until he too was floating, then he paddled toward her unsurely, but she only laughed and splashed at him. They both treaded water and faced each other as swallows swooped in and skimmed the pond for a drink, then swept back into the sky, banking over a stand of scrub oak and dipping into the arroyo out of sight. She splashed him again and ducked below the water, surfacing in the shallows at the far side, rising and turning her bare back to him. Perhaps surprised at her own boldness, she gathered her thick dark hair at the nape of her neck and wrung it. A thin stream trickled down her spine, down her legs.

Like Odysseus on the mast he stayed in the deep water as she turned to him, wavelets lapping at her ankles, everywhere sun-browned except the lower crescents of her breasts and a narrow band crossing her pelvis below her navel and above her tapered thighs. She was a vision escaped from Genesis, incarnating desire in ecstasy soaring upward from a nostalgic premonition of recurring loss and emptiness, vast cycles of wanting and losing and extinguishing and wanting, so beautiful he ached from the center out and he smiled from the pain. Ruby smiled back, further elongating an impossibly stretched moment, a bottomless moment, a pit with no bottom in this world—or a passage. But her pose demanded answer, her precarious offer that he had imagined countless sultry nights alone but never truly expected: to invite him inside, to penetrate that enveloping ecstasy, to plunge into, through, past, to emerge in the presence of, naked and naked with her, squinting into that white-hot light burning within her like a candle, to taste the sweet water dripping from her skin, to hoist her upon him— her offer never voiced and finally expiring as her head turned to follow a far-off sound. She stepped up to the sandy bank and walked with dainty care and an eye for thorns around the shore to her clothes, then left him to paddle around in his own embarrassment and regret. He stared at the spot where she had stood, he stared as though waiting for lightning to strike and they never spoke about it until today.

"But you didn't come to me," she concludes, her eyes now abandoning him. "Because you were afraid of her and she knew it. You couldn't risk your place here."

"You were always the untouchable," he agrees, but he wanted to ask, Who were the exceptions?

"Now she's gone, and I'm free." She steps back, avoiding his gaze, slips out of her overcoat and takes it to the hallway closet.

Before he can decide what to do, what action could possibly be appropriate, she has returned, striding to the refrigerator and hauling out a box of red wine.

"Mom always kept some of this on hand," she says. Daniel fetches two long-stemmed glasses from a cupboard as she sets the box on the counter.

"Don't you think paper cups might be more appropriate?" Ruby jokes.

"Why don't you go sit down?" he suggests, pouring them each a glass before following her into the living room, where he sits beside her on the couch by the big window that faces another broad series of cliffs and the isolated spire of Steeple Rock. The sun settles toward the ridgeline of Mesa de San Francisco.

"I was with her when she found the petroglyphs," Ruby begins, her voice pitched high but unwavering. "I was fourteen, I think. It was a really tough summer for her. She was trying to finish her doctorate so she could lead the dig. Remember? Wasn't that your second summer here? Tomás came back to work for us that year. She hired him to piss off Dad, I swear. There was a site where there'd been a mass slaughter of bison, like in 800 AD. One of the largest discovered kills, Mom said. It was below that barranca where Escalante Creek enters the lake. Anyway . . ."

Ruby falls silent for a moment, staring out the window while the sun quietly floods the room and flows across her face and hair, glittering like jewels in her eyes—she has an affinity for the sun, he realizes, his memories of her are composed primarily in sunshine, the color of her skin and hair dipped from a palette of fluid light such as this, and again he finds it hard to take his eyes off her, though she stares straight ahead outside, stares backward into memory. "We were out walking. She had come into my room after dinner and asked me if I wanted to walk with her. I was at that real rebellious stage, you know? You remember. I'd sneak out to the arroyo to smoke a joint. I was so cool, hanging out with you guys down at the barn. So I thought, I'll be a good girl one more time, and go for a walk with Mom. It was a beautiful evening. It had rained that afternoon, and the smell of juniper filled the air. We walked along the cliffs. At first she was quiet—you know how she could be—and then she talked about me, about how pretty I was, and how I was going to be beautiful, and how men would swarm—that was the word she used, *swarm*.

"She always thought of herself as being very plain. She told me I should never 'have intercourse' until I was married. There we are, walking along the base of the cliffs on this gorgeous night, and the bats and night hawks are starting to dive around us, and we're having the big sex talk. Little did she know. And then she stopped all of a sudden and kind of steadied herself against a rock, like she felt faint, and she'd forgotten all about me and the sanctity of being a virgin. She stood there a minute, she just snapped, and I was getting kind of scared. Then she started walking up this small hill—you can see it from here"—but Ruby doesn't point it out—"and along the base of the cliff she found them, the carvings of the big hand and the wolves. She stood and stared at them a while. It's a hard place to get to because of that drop-off, and I was afraid to follow her. She said"—now Ruby's voice flutters—"she said—and I could barely hear her—she said, 'I remember these.'"

Ruby turns to Daniel. "It sent chills down my spine, it was so spooky. So I went over. Those wolves. I asked her and she said she'd never been there before and I said then how can you remember them? But she kind of waved me away. I remember thinking then that she hated me. When we got home she said she felt a migraine coming on and she hid in her room till the next day. She was so changeable. At night—" Her voice falters, breaking in her throat, the words throttled not by grief, it seems, but anger and other emotions deep beyond his fathoming.

Still Daniel senses a distance between them, a rift of asymmetrical expectation. Uncertainty grips him now as a physical weakness, a numbness in his limbs, and while she stiffens her shoulders he sits apart bewildered, waiting, as usual, for her next move.

"It's like this curtain lowers in front of my eyes." Released and emboldened by her softening tone, he strokes her hair. Now behind the mesa, the sun lights one small cloud, ragged where wind feathers its leading edge, a smoldering red like coals. Her breathing has steadied. Ruby shifts toward him, settling her head to his chest. Into the duskiness of the room she murmurs, "This is nice," her voice modulated to a purr. And after another extended pause, as Daniel again feels that buoyant dizziness and his only touch with the world is the pressing weight of her head against him, the weight of her head, the outline of her nose in the dusky night and the faint scent of flowers like bright points of light on the edge of a dream, a persistent dream seeping with dusk into this room, this girl-now-woman whose head, the pressing weight of her head against him like a bright point of light like Venus out there setting just as it begins to shine setting over the mesa dropping into the scent of flowers, Venus setting out there bright beyond hearing, her voice reels him in. "Stay with me tonight. I can't face this night alone," her head still leaning against him, his fingers brushing her hair, Venus now gone.

He has to think and to wonder before answering, must allow a sudden and involuntary arousal to pass before answering with guilt and some suspicion of his own motives, not hers: "Sure. Of course. Where's your dad and Harvey?"

"I don't know. They should be here by now." Ruby sits upright but still leans against him. "They don't have to know. I'm staying over in the bunkhouse anyhow. I told Dad I won't stay in his house. Ever. It doesn't matter—don't worry about what they'll think. Just stay with me. The nights have been a little rough for me lately."

"Okay," he says, again sensing the stories he hasn't yet heard. A thrill rushes through him, a tingle from proximate danger, that elation he would feel standing at the sheer edge of Capilla Peak peering over and blown slightly off balance by a sudden gust at his back, the elation of risk and sudden insight, the risk of a fulfilled moment, of wholly committing to this moment.

Standing, she adjusts her dress, shifting her hips around in it and smoothing the material against herself, a feminine movement, natural but deliberate, fully conscious of his eyes upon her and performed with the skill that comes of practice: as she walks around the couch behind him she is two, she is desire sheathed in grief, she is the woman abandoning the parents' child.

3.

RUBY HEADS DOWN THE HALLWAY. Daniel steps outside through the front door and is startled to see three dark figures standing in a loose semicircle beneath the cold starlight that reveals only through shadow, not illumination. They stand quietly and motionless, but a ripple spreads outward from them into the silence, pulsating around Daniel, and he pictures their previous words radiating into the night, washing over the outflung arms of Mesa Reina and the summit of Las Animas and her body far out there somewhere, secrets that—once spoken—will vibrate forever yet unrevealed in all that near and distant rock. Into the silence he steps, then, unsure of his footing and still they don't speak or move, so he stops perhaps ten paces away and tilts his head back to gaze starward. He is cold.

Calvin speaks, his voice pitched for no particular ear but aimed wide, the voice of a thought aloud: "There was no forgiveness in her. She didn't forgive us, or herself, for anything. She felt unworthy of this world, of Creation. She saw too much, too much pain. I supposed I've caused more than my share."

He sighs heavily, a whistling exhalation, and Daniel hears Harvey's breath shorten, his throat tightening, but Tomás begins to whistle between his teeth precisely and quietly while the other men grow silent again.

Tomás quits after a moment or two. Daniel notices a pair of shadowy deer grazing in the pasture across the road, two small yearlings tearing at the withered, late-season alfalfa. He looks to the sky again, hoping for a shooting star, but the Milky Way only glimmers dully back at him.

Again Calvin speaks, this time clearly to Tomás. "We need to find those bulls tomorrow. Maybe after all this snow and rain we'll be able to track them."

"Life goes on," Harvey says, his voice still strained.

"What choice is there? If you can't fix it, it's best to move on," Calvin replies, as though he might forestall Harvey's answer, but then the door opens behind Daniel and yellow light leaps from the house into the night, flashing across the ground like fire, and Ruby says, "Daniel?" tentatively, and again he thinks of words vibrating in rock with all the secret tremors of the world harmonizing, his name spoken into the place—

"Yes."

She stands still in the threshold. "Come back in?" but already he is walking to the house, Tomás behind him saying, "We'd better all go in," and when Daniel reaches the door she steps backward, slightly stooped as if under a weight, and she appears small.

"I put some food in the oven," she says. "People have brought so much. They're so generous." She turns sideways in the narrow entryway so he can squeeze by, not looking at him but at the empty air somewhere near his chest. Harvey follows next, stopping by Ruby. They embrace and Daniel looks away, embarrassed, as if he were caught peeping. He walks into the kitchen to check the food, wishing he were gone, half sitting on the counter, staring at the clock, which says six forty-three. Calvin comes in, nods with the tired deacon face to Daniel, runs himself a glass of water, and drinks it slowly without pause. He sets the glass in the sink and turns to Daniel, raising his eyebrows against the futility of speaking, then slowly shaking his head, as if all is hopeless. "This is going to take time, a long time," he says.

Calvin's eyes flick off Daniel to the doorway where Ruby now stands and back to Daniel again. "Are you staying here tonight?" Calvin asks. "You're welcome."

"I'd hoped to—I can sleep out somewhere. I brought my sleeping bag and a tarp. It's no trouble—"

"No, no, there's plenty of space in the bunkhouse. Take your old room. I think there's bedding. Rae kept it ready. . . ."

Daniel nods to keep Calvin from finishing his sentence while Ruby drifts on private currents of thought. "Well," Calvin concludes, glancing at each of them again, picking up a pot holder and bending to open the oven door, then sliding out a platter loaded with ham.

They sit down in the dining room, Daniel across from another broad, west-facing picture window, and despite its dimmed reflection of these people gathering, of Tomás's wife, Criselda, dishing out peas and Harvey slicing bread, of the conspicuously empty chair opposite Calvin at one end of the long pine wood table, despite its dim duplication of this stricken domestic tableau Daniel knows how patiently the desert waits beyond the glass, expansive and surrounding the house and pulling at him in all directions, vast and tugging, the rows on rows of juniper hills building like waves, the winding arroyos as twisted as piñon roots with a single set of coyote tracks drawing him outward where all clocks stop and words still vibrate deep in the stone: precisely there she has come to a final resonant rest. Envying the authority of Rae's departure, he stumbles onto the uncertainty of his life and the agony of playing predicate to Ruby's subject.

"Ham, Daniel?" Tomás is speaking, his voice lilting and musical, adding syllables to his name with a familiar implied irony. Daniel is startled as though awakened and he finds Ruby's eyes steady on him, her lips parted slightly, the teeth white, the eyes narrowed, her skin aglow as from an invisible light, the remembered sun, perhaps, resonating—Daniel is startled as though the drums have quite suddenly stopped—Tomás's face creases into a sympathetic smile under Indian cheekbones, his teeth remarkably white too, his eyes their always-surprising green, the product of a typically New Mexican mixed ancestry.

They eat slowly. Calvin looks from face to face while he chews, observing each with patriarchal concern, yet Daniel finds him reluctant to hold eye contact. Ruby studies her plate. Harvey has found his appetite and cleans off the serving platter. In Spanish, Criselda and Tomás speak softly between themselves as if there's a glass wall between them and the others. The musical rattle and clink of silverware against china plates fills the space between words. The wind has picked up, shaking windows in their casings. The chimney spark suppresser groans as it turns like a windmill in the gusts. Calvin and Harvey discuss the weather, the calves out on the unprotected flats where antelope, like dolphins on a grassy sea, bolt like dolphins bobbing in the waves.

When they are done and have cleared the table and Daniel has helped Criselda wash dishes in the sink and wipe them dry with a dish towel calendar from 1969, Calvin announces to no one in particular that he will go to bed, and Daniel follows Tomás and Criselda outside to their truck. Daniel can't think what to say. He doesn't know Criselda very well and not knowing her suppresses conversation with Tomás.

"This ranch is half mine now," Tomás says finally, cranking the starter.

Daniel is stunned. "You're kidding."

"All we've got to do is find the will. But Rae showed it to me once, we signed it down at the bank with a notary, but I guess she never got it back to Richard Cook." Cook was the family lawyer.

"So you and Calvin going to be partners?"

"Oh, no. Me and Ruby and Harvey."

"Why not Calvin?" Daniel asks, confused.

"Ask Ruby."

Daniel takes this in for a moment, then adds: "Good thing she had it witnessed, huh?"

"There's always a witness, *qué no*, Daniel?" The engine rumbles alive. Tomás swings shut the door, rolls down the window. "Sorry you had to witness all this." Tomás tips his head toward the house, sealing the joke. "Hell, you're part of it too. Don't forget that. Well, we'll see you—" and Criselda calls, "Good-bye!" as the truck lurches forward and rolls crackling over the gravel on the driveway.

Daniel watches the taillights depart, then walks up the hill toward the chapel and his car. The word tumbles over and over in his mind: *witness*. Apart from consequence, neither guilty nor innocent, he sits a moment before twisting the key, loathe to shatter the perfect quiet of the night and reveal his watchful presence to the deer and any other prey finding refuge in the dark.

Finally he starts the car and creeps it down to the bunkhouse. The cedar siding smells woody and damp as he hauls his suitcase out of the trunk and steps onto the creaking porch in front of his old room. When he pulls open the screen door, its spring squeaks like it always did. Behind the bunkhouse the creek rushes full of brown and murky water. As he goes inside, he pictures it swollen bank to bank and the boulders jostling against each other and banged by heavy cottonwood branches washed down from farther up the canyon and he wonders where they can cross the stream by horse in such high water. If it freezes hard tonight in the mountains above the ranch, they won't have to worry.

He goes inside and flips on the bare overhead light. The room is the same as he left it a couple years ago when he moved to the nearby village, then headed for the city to finish college—the bunk beds sagging and narrow as canoes stacked against the north wall, the built-in desk below the polished-metal mirror, and the long shelf above the rod where he would hang his clothes on the south wall. Ask Ruby, he thinks.

Exhaling a cloudy breath, he crouches at the gas heater with a match torn from a cardboard El Rialto Restaurant match-book that was sitting on the window ledge. First he holds the button down for half a minute, like the printed instructions say, then he lights the pilot and kicks on the heat. The flame roars like a waterfall and immediately the warmth spreads over him.

He stands in front of the mirror, studying his reflection, pulling off his tie and the uncomfortable dress shirt and digging into his suitcase for a sweatshirt. His watch says ten. He listens to the turbulence of burning propane and cocks an ear for Ruby's footfall on the porch.

4.

DANIEL HAD COME TO THE RANCH as a fifteen-year-old serving
an exile imposed by his father for a misdemeanor that wasn't
his fault. That sentence turned out to be adolescent paradise,
but as long as it kept him out of trouble, Dad didn't mind.

One Friday night Daniel had been riding in Brad Hale's
Rambler American around Brad's doctors-and-lawyers
neighborhood in Albuquerque. Brad was a year older and
already had his license. People parked their third and fourth
cars along the street, choking the drivable channel down
so two cars barely could pass. Streetlights were few. The boys
had been cruising aimlessly with a couple other friends, trading hits on a joint, laughing at every crude joke they could
think of.

"Man, I'm starving," Brad said. "Anybody up for the Dog
House? Wait! Check it out." As another car approached around
a curve, Brad slowed down and cut off his lights, then flipped
them back on at the last second, honking and yelling out the
window. All the boys gave the astonished oncoming driver
the finger—some old blue-haired lady in a big Buick—and
Hale finally swerved into a gap between parked cars along the
curve. The old lady screeched to a stop. Daniel was laughing so

hard he was having trouble breathing; his buddies, too. Brad gunned away from the curb, yelling, "Watch out," back at the perplexed woman, who must have thought the green Rambler appeared from nowhere.

The trick was so hilarious, Brad repeated it twice, but the third time, he swerved too late and the oncoming pick-up's fender clipped the Rambler's rear quarter in a sickening *graunch* of metal. Brad kept going, whipping the old sedan flat-out from the side street onto a busier artery. The truck, a souped-up Chevy, U-turned in high pursuit. Brad panicked and headed home. The ensuing parental brouhaha ultimately resulted in Daniel's exile to the McCullough Ranch boot camp—at least, that's what his dad imagined the experience would be. He had known Calvin in Korea and thought he might straighten out the boy on the ranch, far from the city's innumerable temptations and opportunities for youthful transgressions.

So he got to be a real cowboy for a summer, and after his parents had deposited him with Calvin, Rae had helped Daniel settle his things in the bunkhouse that first day. Then he had wandered down to the corrals and found this striking girl, so slender and dark, so unlike her fair-haired father, grooming a little bay mustang mare in the cool airy shade of the barn.

Ruby had tied Boca to the hitch post at the open end of the barn and was brushing caked mud from the mare's fetlocks when Daniel had approached her, and she had said, "Hello," still a girl, really, her hair long and straight, and she wore a cowgirl shirt with piping on the back yoke and old torn Levi's. She had continued grooming while he stood and watched her and flies buzzed in the white sun of the barnyard.

"I'm Daniel," he had said with a condescending politeness, then she straightened and dropped her brush into a bucket next to the horse and walked over to him and shook hands with a surprisingly strong grip.

"I'm Maryanne," she said, pointedly looking him in the eye, "but everybody calls me Ruby. I know who you are. You're working here this summer," and her unexpected poise made him take an involuntary step back. "I hope you like it here. Well, I'm going for a ride." She turned, saying somewhat louder over her shoulder, "Nice to meet you," and he sensed the interview was over and he was smitten by her as by a particularly lovely filly, all graceful motion and unconscious beauty, a joyful blooming of spirit in the world, but nothing that can be held, only witnessed, then in later years as they both grew up his idealized admiration of her settled downward and took root, gripped by her emerging sensuality.

He had never seen a girl like her, and that night he imagined her older and undressed, compliant in acts he had only read about but felt sure he would never actually perform—somehow that crucial step of becoming naked with her seemed beyond him, though he hungered for it like a famine victim craves a meal.

Daniel started coming to the ranch every summer, all summer. When Ruby had finished her junior year at prep school and Daniel came back after a year of college, she was in the habit of sneaking out late at night to the bunkhouse to play cards with him and Lester. Daniel still felt like he was on probation at the ranch, trying to stay in Calvin and Rae's good graces, so his actions toward Ruby were often contingent and tentative. He didn't dare jeopardize his position in this magical crazy place or his proximity to Ruby as she came of age. It was better to wait, bide his time. He hadn't imagined then that he might become part of the craziness she was escaping.

He and Lester had kept a cooler full of beer back in those

days and they treated her like a porcelain cup or fine crystal, lovely to see but they were careful not to leave fingerprints, though sometimes, laughing at one of his jokes, she would lean over the cards and lay a hand on his arm and he remembered that touch all night, the weight of her fingers, her hand cold like porcelain, a touch shot through with color, and he lay in bed a long time before falling to sleep, listening to the sprinklers switch-switching on the hay field. Then in the morning Lester rose first, clunking around in the room next door, going outside, walking down the porch to the kitchen, starting bacon in the big iron skillet. And when Daniel joined him, Lester allowed an ironic smile and asked, "Sleep well?" and they both knew he was talking about Ruby. Daniel had dreamed she came to him, slipping into his room, slipping hot into his sheets, dreams so real he awakened, her name whole in his mouth, a physical fullness inside him, her name—

"Daniel?" she calls softly from the porch.

In two steps he reaches the door and pulls it open.

"Hi," she says, sliding past him. She sets a small overnight bag on the desk, hunts through it, and drags out a hairbrush.

He leans against the top bunk, feeling giant, tremendously too large for the room, and it seems she concentrates on not looking at him.

"It's always hard for me to come home," she says into her bag, the brush clutched but forgotten in her hand. "It got so I can't stay in that house. The last couple times I've stayed with Criselda and Tomás. Mom and I would fight and Dad was always lurking . . ." and again Daniel senses a missing scene to this story. "Mom hated that I lived in LA and didn't go to college. Sometimes I'd stay out here in the bunkhouse and remember the fun we had together, you and Les and me. You and me." She sighs heavily and leans over the desk, her arms straight and her weight resting on the heels of her hands, her head bent.

"You must be exhausted," he says, afraid to touch her yet, to hold her, to gather her into his arms.

"How do you feel about me, really?" she asks, still looking downward, her voice as brittle and thin and dry as white October frost. She waits motionless for his reply and he realizes just now, sees in the tense set of her shoulders that she has wanted to ask him this question for a long time, probably for years, and he feels suddenly happy, and nearly contented, and capable of love but alert for sexual opportunity.

"I love you," he says. The words spill out, jostling in a swirling melted flood. "I've always been in love with you, since I first saw you, I guess."

"I think about you all the time," Ruby says, not looking up. "But—we've known each other so long and we never talked this way before. We never quite got all the way down to it. Almost."

"The timing was always wrong. First you were too young, then you had a boyfriend—"

"It's going to be my ranch now, with Harv and Tomás," she interrupts.

"Tomás said." Daniel wants to know more, to ask, Why Tomás? But Ruby turns away from the desk and goes to the bunks, sits on the bottom bed near where he stands. She still owns this conversation. "When Mom died, I looked at my life, at the people I knew, all the guys—it's been wasted. I've really fucked up. I've got nothing to show for nineteen years. I was in Hollywood bed-hopping with a bunch of rock 'n' rollers: that's what Mom thought. And she was right. Well, that's what she got for locking me out. Talk about being thrown to the wolves. Like a sacrificial virgin." She flexes her hands and clasps them together in her lap like praying. Her fingers are long and veined and sinuous with erotic potential. "I'm all cried out, but I feel so terrible. It's like emotional puking."

He sits down beside her and she yawns and he asks, "Do you think you can sleep?"

"Probably. I've got some pills."

"Why don't you take the bottom bunk," he suggests.

She tilts her head onto his shoulder and he nuzzles her hair, imagines a meadow of wildflowers, a jungle of scent—

—bright like Venus, mourning—

—not free of danger, but stalked by wolves, peopled by faceless ancients who dodge among the trees of the margin intimately familiar, craving but afraid of the light, choosing instead the wolves, becoming the wolves—

A coyote yaps from across the arroyo. Ruby starts in surprise, then settles against him and squeezes his knee while the barks continue. "It startled me," she whispers. "When I was a girl, I used to imagine I was a coyote. Sometimes I'd go off alone on walks and I'd follow their trails, and I'd think: this is what a coyote would do. Remember *The Call of the Wild*? I read it twenty times, probably. I loved that scene at the end where Buck trots off into the woods with the wolf: that was me, I thought."

—stalked, then stalking—

"I was always a lion, a cougar," he admits.

"Yes," she agrees. "You're definitely a cat."

—turning the tables—

"Kind of sneaky . . ."

"Ha!" she laughs.

"Crouched down in the grass, ears flat . . ."

"Oh!"

". . . watching."

"Yes!"

Another coyote joins the first, a voice more distant, wild and howling, sadly lunatic. Then a full chorus of yip-yip-yipping and crazy barks ripping apart the fabric of darkness, ripping apart the logic of thought, even, while Daniel sits with Ruby in awe, sits with the stillness of piety, sits in reverence before the outrageous expressiveness of the world, the knowing crazy voices of the night ripping apart all the tiny threads holding him to—

"My mother is out there somewhere," Ruby whispers, and Daniel feels the hairs rising on the back of his neck. "I know what my dad did. . . . I need to know where she is. It would be in her journals, those diaries she kept. Then everyone would know I'm not crazy, that I'm telling the truth about what happened to me. They would explain everything. Until then—it's like limbo. I can't get on with stuff."

The coyotes have stopped, but the night is transformed: coyotes will find her corpse, circle beneath the scaffolding with whining impatience, sometimes jumping against one of the vertical corner posts, pawing at it, wishing for hands, free in the night to reclaim her, to drag her back into a dark corner of sandstone, fearless of discovery. Again for an instant he envies Rae's departure, its promise of revelations denied him, that fearless reclaiming.

His arm around Ruby hugging her close, they gently rock side to side, her breathing steady, then she separates from him and stands, turning stiffly away, her eyes strangely unfocused, her voice detached. "I'm going to change." At the door her body reanimates with lithe, studied sensuality, her hips swaying to one side, her long fingers stroking the doorknob—"Wait up for me"—her tongue flicking over teeth as she twists away and out the door.

She—

—goes out to the porch then, carrying her bag, his life now summarized by this tiny room in the bunkhouse, the redwood porch, the bathroom with its shower and plywood toilet stall and two sinks where she now changes into pajamas and brushes her hair—or so he imagines—and gathers it at the base of her neck, splashing cold water on her face while he waits still captivated by her presence, her return as a presence in his life erasing the elapsed years of waiting, of wondering, of wanting—

She—

—who shimmers like a mirage in the unlit corner of his dreams, as silent as night, never quite forgotten nor fully recalled, but sensed like a glowing warmth on skin, the nebulous field levitating a thought or like an awareness of gravity, that relentless inescapable pull toward the center—

—while he strips down to his underwear and the black east window reveals nothing of the night but reflects him instead, and he turns down the gas heat, then sits on the bottom bunk and leans against the wall, pulling the musty old army blanket over his legs and the bedsprings sagging in the middle like a canoe.

He waits.

Like every other clue, the coyotes are gone and he cannot hear the stream in the arroyo over the low fluttering of the heater's pilot flame, nor can he hear any sign of her return, but as he loses reckoning of the flow of time he wonders if he mistook her intent and he begins to worry, to imagine she sits huddled in a corner on the floor, hugging her knees to her chest crying in the stark fluorescent light on the garish yellow linoleum crying, hugging her knees to her chest, crying against the insufferable anguish of separation and loss while her mother—

—who slips atom by atom into place—

—returns:

"I'm back," she announces in a low whisper, in a gauzy gown her transformation from mourning daughter to seductress complete. Ruby closes the door deliberately but softly as if it were important not to disturb the night, which gallops away from them in silence like field mice on snow, silent and scattering to every horizon and infinitely upward too, then inward: the dark corners. He sits up and thinks for something to say that will clarify this moment, restore its continuity with the rest of his life, make sense of this unpredicted moment to which henceforth every other moment will refer, to fix it in time and memory with words, to negotiate this moment into a contract with her, saying: It started there, remember? That was when we began together. Before that—

"Thank you," Ruby breathes, a lilt lifting each word into implied promise, and seeing the question of his face, adds, "for waiting."

"Just now?" he asks. "Or the last six years?"

"I was afraid you might be asleep." She glides to the edge of the bed. The bare overhead light is harsh behind her, too bright, as if she were onstage with her body, as if this were a show for him, and he wonders who else, how many others, have caught her act. The thought sticks thornily in his head as her hand floats to his face and her eyes glaze into a metallic stare skidding off to the side. Her long fingers stroke across his cheek and he kisses her palm, while her left hand begins stroking him up and down in a determined rhythm and her tongue dances in his mouth. Now his fingertips skate onto her bare legs, gliding upward, but when his hand finds her inner thigh, she stops everything. Her whole body stiffens. He takes her hand as it withdraws from his face and he kisses the back of it before returning it to her. Though nearly overcome with lust, he feels the moment pivot away from consummation and he thinks, How could she do it now, anyway? This sexual yo-yo-ing is familiar enough to ride a bit longer.

Ruby gathers the gown across her chest and steps in confusion toward the door, grabs the handle, drops it again as she turns back to him. "You must think I'm out of my fucking mind," she says, her voice deep in her throat, each word chiseled square into a stone block, a wall dividing the night between where it was heading and where it has arrived, no more of that breathy tempting lilt pitched to a man's desire.

"Maybe I should sleep in Lester's old room," Daniel offers, sitting up, wondering if he's found the fulcrum to tip her back toward him.

As if she didn't hear him, she says, "What if you could never have me? Would you still love me? Or better yet, will you still love me after I've fucked your brains out? Will you still even be able to look at me?" Her hand grabs the knob again and twists it lightly back and forth: Go? Stay? Go?

She stays.

"Do you want to talk?" he asks, easing into the gelded role of confidant so he can stay close, though where the sublimated lust blends into sincere compassion is beyond his reckoning. Balancing forces of anticipation and doubt hold him in a tight orbit around her.

Ruby clicks off the light. "No."

Even in the dark she asks him to look away so she can change into a T-shirt. He gives her the bottom bunk and scrambles by feel onto the top. The frame creaks under his weight.

A little while later, as time begins to seep outward into the darkness and he expands with the night, she adds, "I do love you, Daniel. I should tell you that. I haven't told you before."

Lying on his side in the room blued by the pilot light, he can't even hear her breathing. He closes his eyes and sees again Turk on the day he left the ranch. He had turned the horse out on pasture and watched him gallop off toward the herd with his head high and nostrils wide, his tail straight up in the air, his hooves thrumming across the sandy earth.

Abruptly he is dreaming, a plunge into awareness like curtains lifted, the stage lights flicked on bright and colorful, dreaming of a parking lot in town under midday sun, a bronze amulet in his hand, the spiraling pattern of intricate runes revealing—a Rosetta stone revealing—or, rather, clarifying in complete and final illumination the most thorough truth—while a strange red car approaches, then he is at the ranch, scrambling down a dry watercourse, climbing over boulders and twisting sideways to slip through water-cut gaps in the rock. Jumping the stagnant brown pools left by the last flood, he is fleeing an unnamed danger in an empty land, a land at peace but for his fear of pursuit: he sees her, across the parking lot, getting out of the car and waiting for him as a deep buzzing hum vibrates the bones of his head: he looks down at the charm in his hand, intent to memorize its intricate truth-telling pattern, as she comes toward him to take it, reaching, the buzzing deepening and spreading a leaden fear throughout his body so that he can't move, like a rabbit turned to stone by fear, while the buzzing hum—

—awakens him, and as he steps through that threshold to consciousness he realizes the sound is himself, moaning. He sits up. Night still inhabits the room. "Ruby?" he whispers, but she does not answer and he lies there a while certain that she is gone until he hears a slight rustling from the covers below, and finally his heartbeat begins to calm and his awareness leaks back out through the walls into the expanding night. The dream was about Rae.

5.

WHEN HIS EYES OPEN AGAIN, a pastel predawn glow fills the room. Ruby is gathering things from the little desk into her handbag. He sees the lacy sheer nightgown stuffed into her overnight bag and wonders why she brought it to her mother's funeral.

"Good morning," he manages, his voice croaky with sleep, and she looks up at him. Her face has aged overnight, or simply fallen, collapsing into another state between anger and grief. Perhaps it is despair, or the blank resignation that comes from emptying out and finding there's nothing left to give up.

"Hi."

"How did you sleep?"

"Oh, I slept." She comes over to him. "Thanks for keeping me company. How odd it must seem. I never thought we'd sleep in separate beds on our first night together." She smiles then, her eyes hooding reflexively in suggestive nuance, but that's the last she'll say about the matter.

He studies the new lines on her face and remembers her as a girl that first summer, her unfettered joy, how she could laugh without complication at little things and they would roar together over their parodies of adult life and grown-up hypocrisy. Her eyes could narrow with precocious mischief then too. Something had changed by the time he saw her again the next summer. She was fifteen then and as developed as a college girl and she rarely laughed out loud. Her sense of playful mischief hid behind a new wariness.

"I'll be happy again—I know that," she says.

"I thought the world of your mom," he says, his voice stiffening as he speaks.

"I know." She sighs, another in an endless series. "She really enjoyed you. She was pretty disappointed when you moved off the ranch last year, I know that. She hated to see you go."

"I remember how she'd bring the posole and tortillas and coffee out onto the flats during roundup: these great steaming vats of posole, and those old enamel coffeepots—I see they're still in your kitchen—hung over a fire. She really knew how to do it. We'd come riding up all grubby and she'd have another big aluminum lidded pot full of hot water and a couple bars of Ivory floating around in it, and she'd yell at anybody who didn't wash up first. And I'd usually sit and eat with Calvin, and she'd stand near us and watch the other guys go through the line, serving, you know. It was the best food, ever. Usually she'd bring her horse"—Ruby is nodding in shared memory, he thinks—"and ride with us that afternoon. While we gathered cattle, she'd tell me what they knew about the Indians who had hunted this valley—when? Fifteen hundred years ago. . . . Is this hard for you?"

"No. I feel so numb, like I'm watching all this happen to another person. What I saw at the service was that there are all these people who had pieces of my mom too, who had all these experiences with her and loved her too, I guess. When you grow up, you realize that about your parents, I think, that there are other people out there who they are important to, who need them, who have them in ways you can't, and keep you from them too. Or they keep themselves away . . ." She goes quiet.

An intimate silence occupies the air around them. Into this atmosphere of opportunity he begins: "Ruby," he says, and he feels slightly breathless, flushed, charmed, her name an incantatory utterance, the magical release into desire beyond risk or responsibility, the stepping across, the giving over to, abandoning what came before, merely her name, casting a web, a spell an affirmation of—she—who—"I . . ."—something that cannot be spoken, nothing.

Her eyes are brown pools as liquid as dreams and oracular, a star setting into that erotic ocean of the primal world, a world without duties or obligations, without these impossible distances and voiceless longings. Aloof but gently mocking, she watches a moment, drawing him into further excess, then coaxing him so softly it's almost a whisper: "What?"

"You are—" he begins again, and the words as he speaks flare brightly with promise but extinguish themselves like sparks popping from a fire, then burning out before reaching the top of their arc. The bright flash, the auspicious upward leap to extinction, the cinder dropping harmless to the ground: so his words seem to die somewhere in the space surrounding Ruby. Still her eyes coax, expectant, not hunting but actively receptive, drawing him inward, teasingly sluttish, and he thinks of loving her now, here, on this bunk, how her knowing hands would guide him in and he thinks she would blow him apart, she would steal him away, he would never return, she would spirit him away to a night garden of flowers and a candle burning, her hair glinting gold, her eyes shimmering, expectant, mute: they leave him, dropping as if to regard the ash, the cinder.

"Let's not talk now," she says in the stone voice from last night, the voice he's never heard before. "Everything's so stirred up." She steps to the mirror, mechanically brushes back her hair with her fingers, looks out the window. "I can't remember the last time I woke up before dawn. 'Bed is your milieu,' as Mom would say. She always got up really early, you know, at least when she hadn't been up all night." Again, the sigh. Ruby leans against the bunk, and he swings his legs over the side, feeling a bit self-conscious in his underwear, but she makes no sign of noticing.

"Have you eaten?" he asks, wondering if she's been to the main house yet.

"I don't eat breakfast."

"How about coffee?" he tries. "I know I need a cup."

"Dad and Harv are probably up," she says as if answering him. "They'll probably go feed horses soon. I better go to the house and fix them something. Will you come with me?"

"Sure, I gotta eat. Give me a few minutes. I need to shower."

"I'll wait." She sits down on the bottom bunk and examines the backs of her hands. "My skin gets so dry here." She rubs them together. "I don't want to go into that house alone. It's okay out here. But in the house—" and Ruby shakes her head. "You know, when we were kids, Harvey and I thought it was haunted, especially that back room Mom uses as a study. It was my bedroom for a while, when I was about eleven or twelve. One night I woke up because I heard someone calling my name." Her face clouds a moment, then she finds the memory's direction again. "At first I thought it was my dad. I heard it so clearly. I remember sitting up, and it was so dark. I looked out the window, and out in the field was this girl, and she was waving to me, like she wanted me to follow her.

I wasn't scared. You know what I thought? I thought: That's me. I'm dead and that's me. I've never told anybody this, except Harvey. She had long dark hair, like me. I don't even remember going back to sleep that night. Why do I tell you these things?"

He shrugs, but he wants to say: It's because you love me—he wants her to say it.

"But I don't tell you everything," she finishes.

He pulls a towel from his suitcase.

"Go ahead. I'll wait," she repeats, and he sticks his bare feet into a pair of moccasins and puts on a coat for the chilly walk down the veranda to the bathroom.

"Come down and talk to me if you want." He pulls the door open and steps outside and is immediately struck by the smell of a desert morning: damp sage and juniper and sand, and the clarity of the air—he smells that too—and again the cedar siding of the porch. He doesn't hear her following, but he heads straight for the shower. The stall is wet so he knows she has preceded him. When the water blasts on—a bit too cold at first, so he jumps back and bends slightly at the waist—his nose wrinkles at the strong sulfur smell; then it turns hot and he dunks his head under and lets the water run all over him, his eyes closed, still not fully awake, so he is startled when he hears her thin voice, only slightly husky: "I'm here." He thinks: Is she standing there with her arms folded and staring at the floor or pacing along in front of the sinks, even fixing her hair or checking how red her eyes are? He notices a slight acceleration in his own blood flow and a shameful wondering passes through him: why does her anguish provoke his desire? He feels compelled to draw out from her every secret, every nuance of her suffering in some final demonstration of intimacy.

"Can I ask you something?" Her voice is just the other side of the wooden shower door.

"Yeah," he says, sensing a shift in strategy.

"Do you have a girlfriend?"

"I go out sometimes."

"I bet you do. Nobody special? A good-looking guy like you?"

He doesn't want to answer, doesn't want to say anything that might imply a limit on his availability to her. "There's this girl named Kate."

"Ah," Ruby answers.

"I'm going to stop seeing her."

"Does she know that yet?"

He lets the water run on him some more and intentionally suppresses an image of Ruby in the shower with him, her sleekness, the wet hair and long fingers. "Yes. No. Not really. Jesus. It doesn't matter. It's done, really, over."

"Is it because of me?" Ruby asks.

"Well . . . no, it's been coming. Lots of things have been building up. I don't think I ever loved her—ever knew what love really was."

"What's she like?"

"Ruby—"

"I'm just curious. Is she pretty?"

"Yeah. She's a dance major."

"Why is it over?"

He starts to lather his hair from a shampoo sample bottle Ruby must have left behind. "We're not . . . we're not compatible. We're hard on each other. We want really different things. She's moving to New York, I think. She's too good to stay here. She's too good. I don't guess I was ever really attracted to her."

"And what do you want that you can't get from a beautiful ballet dancer?" Ruby presses, a hint of wise irony brightening her voice.

"You," he returns without pause: it is the only acceptable answer, as her silence affirms. Her vanity has always excited him, her awareness of that inner hold she has on him, those long fingers reaching in, and he knows how her eyelids would half close and like a gypsy with all the cards she would watch him, even shove him along down that helpless slide, that avalanche beginning in his toes and gathering along his veins and in his bones, the implosion like worlds colliding at the apex of their union: she would watch him fly over the edge. He knows she knows, she is standing on the other side of the shower door like a conductor with a baton, counting off the beats of his heart. So instead he dials in more cold and lets the water chill him.

Sex was not discussed in Daniel's family. He was unprepared for the feelings that surged through him the summer after he turned twelve, the frequent erections, the sudden riveting fascination he found in women's bodies. His parents seemed to inhabit an asexual world—his mother at home with her cigarettes and daytime TV, his father gone days and sometimes into the night to his gray-suit office—and neither was even remotely inclined to discuss with him how he might vent this pubescent heat. His mother would cluck disparagingly at Catwoman's latex bodysuit or Jeannie's I-dream-of-cleavage harem outfit. Mom said, "You don't need to be seeing that," and turn the channel to something more innocuous. When his mother changed his bed and discovered *Playboy* under his mattress, she erupted in righteous rage, confiscating the offending material, calling Brad Hale's mom (after Daniel confessed where he got the magazine), and uttering that most chilling threat: "Just wait till your father gets home."

So Daniel played with the dog in the yard the rest of the afternoon, but when his father came home and summoned him into his bedroom for the dreaded patriarchal ass-chewing, all Dad said was, "This kind of material is wholly inappropriate and I expect you to never bring it home again." So Daniel left with the intriguingly ambivalent sanction to find his stimulation away from home. Out of sight, out of trouble.

Because Daniel went to an all-boys prep school, he had little opportunity to experience three-dimensional girls. When Brad Hale got his license, they would cruise the local McDonald's, the open-air mall, the public high school football games, where the cheerleaders doing their high kicks in microskirts sketched a whole week's worth of turbulent imagery. Sometimes a cute girl in a halter top might return his lingering stare with a brief eye lock, but he lacked the confidence or skill to engage her, though he'd return to McDonald's on the next weekend hoping to see her again. But it never happened.

"I'm sorry," she says, not apologetically but wistfully, "for being such a wreck," and he wonders if she can see through the door. "I think about making love to you—I have this little fantasy of how it would be—and now we're together and I can't. . . . It's like all the switches are off." Her voice is getting smaller. "Can you wait for me? Am I worth it?" A strained urgency pinches the words into a breathy plea.

"Of course you are," he insists immediately and ineffectually, the words as weak as clouds against volcanic fire.

"Yeah? What if you find out I'm not. Where will you be then?"

He cuts off the water and asks: "Are you all right? Ruby?"

"As all right as I've ever been."

He grabs a towel and steps out of the shower. She holds her face with her hands and shakes her head, shakes her head, even while he holds her, shaking her head, the pain passing between them skin to skin, and he sees the darkness that she sees, the visions, or memories, from which there is no rest or relief—

—windows, misted—

—and an echoing shriek that ascends the register of human hearing until it is a kind of howl echoing off the moon, and coming back empty, a hollow sound like the scraping noise of paws with hard nails scratching frantically against wood.

"How soon do you have to leave?" Ruby asks back at the room as he tugs on his boots, sitting on the bunk beside her. It is almost seven o'clock.

"Soon. I've got a class at noon, and it's a two-hour drive." He stands. "Ready to go up to the house?" He holds out his hand to help her up and she takes it but stays sitting and looks at him, her head tilted slightly to the side and back to regard him. "Why does it seem like you and I are always saying good-bye? I think sometimes that we're supposed to be apart, fated." She sighs but not from that crater of despair; something less. "It's funny: I go away, you go away. Then we see each other and it's like we've never been apart."

"It's funny," he says, but with irony, which she acknowledges with a squint before pulling against his hand to rise. "Let's go," he says.

The day is clear and Daniel can feel the sun drawing moisture from the sandy road. Ragged, misty clouds hang about Mesa Reina to the north, but already the sun is burning them up. "It's going to be a beautiful day," he observes.

"Um-hum," she returns, and her arm finds its way around his waist so she can lean on him as they walk and fill him with that euphoria of contact.

"I haven't asked you—" he starts.

"What?"

"If you're still seeing David."

She squeezes at his waist but doesn't answer at first. While he waits, he notices that the alfalfa field along the road was recently cut. He remembers mowing it in high summer, that rich, almost edible smell and the sickle on the tractor chewing through it, sometimes snagging a little rabbit that doesn't know where to run, and once Daniel had felt he couldn't keep mowing—the dead rabbits—but the sun warm on his back too, the tractor purring along, and he'd lift the blade for each turn, spinning the tractor on one wheel to the outside of the corner and swinging the teeth down to cut the next swath.

"I suppose I am," she answers after some reflection. "I've seen a few guys. They don't mean anything to me. Sometimes I think I can't live without a man around. Some man. Any man. Isn't that awful? But I'm a strong person. I am. I don't feel dependent on them, exactly. I don't know. . . . It's irrational. I enjoy the sex—I don't think there's anything wrong with that. I'm a sexual person. I know that about myself. And then they start hanging around, and I get tired of them. But there are men, and then there are *men*. I seem to attract—sleazy guys. Like, there was this one—I met him through my girlfriend—who wanted me to be in movies. You know the kind of movies. . . . I went over with her to his house one night, for drinks, and he put this videotape in the machine and said he wanted to show us a movie he had made. So I'm sitting there, enjoying a margarita, and he sits down next to me, and these people start fucking on the screen. It was really too much. I told him I wasn't interested and got the hell out of there. But I think: Why me? It's like I've got 'easy' stamped on my forehead. There's always some guy knocking on the door."

"Is that what I'm doing?" he asks, insistence creeping into his voice.

She stops then and keeps looking at her feet in their antiseptic white exercise shoes. "No. No—you're already in."

"I'm sorry," he says, "I don't mean to press."

"I know—"

They start walking again.

"So when are you moving back?" he asks.

"I'm not. I'm just staying long enough to tie up some loose ends, to have a talk with Dad. It's hard to imagine living here. I can't bear the thought of it. I keep thinking: I must be dreaming. My mother can't be dead. This can't really be happening. The way Mom left it—I don't know all the details yet—it's like she divorced Dad in her death and he gets nothing. You gotta admit, that takes some balls. She didn't have 'em when she was alive, though." But Ruby's mood won't stay down, or she needs to keep Daniel on the line. "We should go away somewhere—you and me—a desert island, with white sand beaches, you know? And blue, blue water, and we could lie around and sunbathe and make love whenever we wanted. Wouldn't that be nice?" Again she is teasing. Her mood swings storm through and turn back on themselves then subside without warning, like the weather. She sags against him so their legs rub as they walk.

"Aw, leave me alone," he protests, and she laughs and pushes him away. They have reached the back door of the house, and he lets her lead inside, then adds: "Anytime, Ruby, anytime. You know that."

But as he pours a cup of coffee from the pot that Calvin probably made before heading out for chores, she says, "I've got a few things to settle first."

6.

HARVEY DRAGS INTO THE KITCHEN, his hair wild under a big ol'
black Stetson so stained and dusty it looks pale gray.

"Mornin'," he says, nodding generally in their direction.
Ruby steps over and kisses him on the cheek and he gives her
a little hug.

"I remember when you got that hat," Daniel says to him.

"Oh, yeah," Harvey returns, pulling it off for a look. "The
Chama Rodeo. I rode the bulls. 1975. I was fourteen, but I
looked older, so they let me ride."

"I remember. You didn't do too bad."

"I stayed on and that was about all," Harvey says wearily.
"The hard part was gettin' off. I didn't make it to the buzzer."

They sit down at the table with their cups. "I got so drunk
that night, and Mom was so pissed, I thought she'd never talk
to me again. You and Les too. You guys drove me home."
Daniel nods along with him while Ruby fusses at the stove.
"We went over to Foster's and I said I wanted to get drunk on
Heinekens, and at first they weren't gonna serve me, cuz I was
underage. Then Lester told them he was my legal guardian—"

"Hey, we had to think of something. . . ."

Ruby is laughing. "His guardian? I never heard that one before. Where was I that day?"

"It was the Fourth of July," Harvey explains.

"Oh. I don't remember it," she says.

"You were partying," Harvey says.

"Undoubtedly," she agrees. "I'm going to see if Dad's here," and she heads off toward his bedroom.

After she has gone, after her footsteps have beat lightly down the carpeted hallway, Harvey looks at Daniel and says, "Are you and Ruby going to get together this time?"

Daniel shakes his head as if the entire problem were beyond reckoning. "Beats me. Should we?"

"Hell, yes," Harvey says. He shoves away from the table abruptly. "Let's go feed horses."

Daniel stands too while Harvey sticks his head into the hallway to tell Ruby, who seems to have disappeared. "Well, let's go," he says.

Into Harvey's old Ford pickup they climb and drive to the barn to pick up several bales of hay. The haystack is tall and vast from a good hay crop this year. The bales smell clean when Daniel, balancing up near the rafters, throws them into the truck bed. After tossing down three he pauses to catch his breath, leaning against a two-by-eight joist while Harvey punches buttons on the radio.

"Are you going to school today, Harv?" Daniel asks as they drive the still-slick road to the home pasture, a wide, flat meadow that spreads all the way to the highway from the cliffs and the small ragged hills and arroyos that clutter their feet.

"Nah."

"How are you doing?"

"I'm doin'," he says. "I didn't sleep at all last night. Not one fuckin' wink. I'm gonna get good and drunk tonight. You be here?"

"I'm leaving this morning."

"Why don't you stay?"

"Gotta go to class, man."

"Ruby—"

"Ruby," Daniel admits.

As they drive the road, the cliffs on their right reveal a series of facets and folds cleaving their face. Daniel studies the darkened apron painted over a V-shaped fissure near the top of the cliffs where water spills in a gushing cascade during especially torrential rain and stains the rock for a hundred feet. Maybe a half-dozen times he and Harvey have hunted around the base of those cliffs for a chimney they could climb, but this face is unscalable. The petroglyphs guard their base and he has always felt watched as he prowls the sandy hills beneath, not only by the startlingly aerial grasshoppers or the occasional terror of a rattlesnake, but—

—a presence, such as might hold a small stone in its hand, chipping, pecking, tracing the strange visions of the soul, while the days roll one onto another and the bones of ancient fish embedded in sandstone swim to the sun, migrating through millennia to betray the apparent solidity of rock, which is merely a trick of time and inattentive vision—

—and at last they would give up and Harvey would say, "Let's get out of here."

"This place can really get under your skin," he says to Harvey. "It gets in your blood."

"Isn't that the truth?"

"When I'm gone, I sort of pine away for it, like it was a person."

"You know what Mom would have said about that . . ." Harvey says.

"What?"

Harvey is silent for a moment, then explosively bangs the flat of his hand against the steering wheel with tremendous force and they hear a crack. He keeps driving, but Daniel can sense a contained violence, an emotional sizzling as though sparks might soon fly across the air between them and set him too afire.

"Well," Daniel begins preventively, "she would have said something, anyhow."

The road follows the fence line of the pasture now, its smooth wire strands gleaming wet. The horses are scattered across the meadow, some out of sight in small draws or deep arroyos, noses to the ground, tearing the well-cured grass. Daniel can't spot Turk.

"Sometimes people can't believe that Ruby and I are brother and sister," Harvey says, letting the truck roll to a stop alongside the fence. "Tomás always says I'm Dad's son, and Ruby is Mom's daughter. But that's not really true. We're both. When I look inside, I see Mom staring back out. But you know what's strange? When I try to picture Mom's face now, all I see is Ruby. We were looking at old pictures of her last night, Dad and me, after you and Ruby had gone to bed"—Daniel feels a blush heating his face—"and it's incredible how much Ruby looks like Mom did when she was younger. I never noticed that before. She sure don't look like Dad, though."

Harvey opens his door and—stepping out—sticks two fingertips into his mouth and whistles shrilly. Several horses jerk up their heads and scan for a moment until they spot the truck. They consider the two men for a moment, then begin a quick walk toward them, others falling into line behind. Two yearlings break from the pack, loping off on a diagonal, shaking their heads and striking out with their front feet as they run.

"Look at those two," Harvey says. The entire herd starts to lope then, a band of mares spreading out for running room, still a quarter mile off but charging toward the men at the fence, and then from nowhere, it seems, Turk appears, exploding whole from the earth like Athena from Zeus's head, bolting out of some small draw or ripple in the meadow where they couldn't see him, galloping away from the herd, bright coppery red in the morning sun, his head high and to one side, whinnying wild and shrill, galloping on his toes so he hardly touches the ground, streaking across the land like some catastrophic eruption of power, an overflowing, a hardening of energy into matter, and first the two yearlings veer off to follow him, then the whole band, circling now away from the fence and back toward the center of the meadow, whinnying and kicking at each other and rumbling the ground like an earthquake, and Daniel feels a welling of tears in his eyes as he and Harvey stand and stare. The horses approach the far fence, perhaps a half mile south, and begin a broad curve, Turk still way out in front, and circle back toward the truck.

As Turk and the two lead mares lope in, Harvey calls, "Whoa, now—take it easy!" and he holds up his hands to ward them off the fence, but it almost looks like a benediction; then he pulls a bale from the back of the truck while the horses mill around, waiting to be fed but too excited to be still.

"Turk!" Daniel calls, and the gelding's head swings around to look at him, his eyes huge and his ears pegged forward. "Hey, buddy!" Daniel ducks through the wires and approaches the horse, who stands quiet but leans his head away and snorts, the whites of his eyes showing; he lets Daniel slap him on the neck a few times. "He looks good," Daniel calls to Harvey.

"Yeah. He ought to," Harvey says, tossing a bale over the fence for Daniel to open. "He's got all this pasture, and we feed 'em, too." Daniel yanks the wire off the bale and spreads the hay around in piles while the horses jostle and threaten each other, but Turk stands apart, his flank quivering slightly from all the running—the very air seems to shimmer with the energy of the horses, that collective power, an overbrimming vitality that might at any moment spill, a deluge of demons, a riptide, unrepressed—and a strangeness, too, and though Daniel has spent years around horses, he again senses their otherness, their connection, their link to something remote, that distant origin, a vast savanna to roam, space without time, an infinity of completion, all the hooves pounding in utter pandemonium.

"When were you up here last?" Harvey asks.

"What was it? Labor Day? That's too long, though, too long. I must be crazy to be living down there."

"Must be," Harvey agrees, and they share a laugh, but Daniel sees the fresh wound in Harvey's eyes, not haunted like Ruby's but crippled by impotent rage against irreversible consequence.

"I keep expecting to see her," Harvey says, the words releasing his tears. "I can't get it through my head. I hear her voice. Last night, I heard her say my name, like she always said it, I could swear it." He is having trouble talking but he presses on. "At the burial yesterday, Ruby said she's still here, she's around. She said Mom could never leave this place."

Turk's jaw muscles flex with each chew while the sun glows red, then redder still on the cliffs below Mesa Reina, and all trace of yesterday's brief snow vanishes into vapor. A small flock of piñon jays swoops among a cluster of trees near the arroyo by the western edge of the pasture; they chatter and scream, the males bright blue, the females a dull gray. The horses have settled down to serious eating.

"It would sure be nice to get out for a ride," Daniel says after a while.

Harvey nods. "Why don't you stay another day?"

Turk's eyes are nearly closed as he eats, those big jaw muscles flexing. "Yeah. I will."

Back at the house they find Tomás's truck—all spattered with mud, even on the roof—and the kitchen smells of bacon as Daniel goes in. Ruby is cooking at the stove while Tomás and Calvin lean over cups of coffee and the room echoes with emptiness, a ringing like the head feels after a tremendous blow; this is how Calvin sits, in shock, motionless, leaning forward onto his elbows, while across from him Tomás sags in his chair, his arms on the table, his legs spraddled far out onto the floor as though exhausted, and it occurs to Daniel that they were out all night and have only now returned. They waste few words on each other. It's part of the pact they must have made a couple decades earlier.

Daniel looks to Ruby, who will not look at him. Harvey walks through the kitchen and down the hallway and Daniel hears the bathroom door close. Ruby's hand is poised over a frying pan full of eggs, a spatula in her hand, which quivers and is noticeable for being the only motion in the room now. Daniel wishes intently that none of this were happening, that he were lying in bed with Ruby and the sunshine rolling down upon them and a damp sogginess—perhaps he were even still inside her and the world were slowly creeping back upon them, with regret but inevitable, like tides eroding their solitude and drawing them back—

"Can I help you?" he says, standing behind her and reaching to take the spatula from her hand and running his fingers down the length of her forearm for the sensation of her skin against his and she shakes her head once "no" so he releases her but stays close.

"It'll be ready in a minute," she says quietly—

—as if not to disturb the dead.

And gradually the room fills, life returns again, Calvin stirring in his chair and taking a sip of coffee.

"Are you going to ride with us, Daniel?" Tomás asks.

Ruby looks a question at him as he begins to answer. "I thought I'd stay today," Daniel replies obliquely, postponing commitment until he has spoken with her, answered her silent query, and Tomás studies him a moment but says nothing more. Daniel senses two, maybe three unspoken conversations around him.

Ruby serves up the breakfast as though she does it every morning of her life, lining up the plates on the counter, then going along and spooning out the scrambled eggs and setting down shriveled crispy strips of bacon and fishing out the toast from the toaster oven, then carrying the plates over to the table for the men, including Harvey, who has returned and is thoroughly expressionless, as though he never intends to speak again. They all pull up to the small round table, even Ruby with only a glass of orange juice. Before they begin to eat, Calvin says, "Let us pray," bowing his head. "Oh, Lord, we are thankful for this food . . ." but Ruby doesn't close her eyes, merely sits quietly with a hand on her glass and watches her father, observing him with interest, as an anthropologist might study a strange ritual.

Her skin is clean and clear and shining, her eyes bright and active. She is radiant with a secret energy, a power of knowledge as though she were the one to bestow this blessing, to grant a wish, to condescend from the heavens and alleviate all suffering with a graceful sweep of her long hand, to guide them away, an exodus to her hidden garden beyond the wild calls and night cries of predators, who even now, Daniel supposes, are dismantling the framework, gnawing at the stilts holding it all up, no longer frantic but methodically dismantling the props holding the corpse up to the sky as ravens circle and sometimes settle on a treetop nearby to watch and comment, free from the great weight of time, which bows their heads at the breakfast table—

"Amen," Daniel says in unison with the others, while Ruby's lips barely move, parting perhaps only for a breath.

Breakfast is silent with the implicit truce except for passing the half-and-half, the salt, the jam. Calvin finishes first. As he pushes back from the table he is about to speak to Ruby, thinks better of it, carries his plate over to the sink. Harvey and Tomás follow, and Daniel stays seated while Ruby waves the other men out of the kitchen, saying, "I'll do all this. You get going . . ." and they leave, Tomás calling back to Daniel: "Grab Turk while he's still in eating, if you want, Dan," then pulling the door shut hard and in a moment they hear the truck start and it passes the kitchen window with her father, her brother, and the other crowded together in the cab.

"It's the matter of her will," Ruby says.

Daniel nods that he understands. "Tomás said something."

"She left out Dad, totally. And there's more. Stuff Harvey doesn't even know. Stuff Dad doesn't think I know."

That's all she seems prepared to say now. "Do you want to ride with the others?" he asks. "We could."

She seems to mull this before answering, "Yes. I want to go out and look for the journals, the will, for Mom, for the place Dad left her."

—scratching and—dismantling—as if the world itself might even be pulled apart.

"How could he do that?" she says with sudden anger, pulling away and turning her back to him. "It makes her—It's like he's saying she was a—That she was—It's like there's a wooden stake stuck in her." Ruby is trembling now. "If I can just see it."

"I need to make a call if I'm going to stay," Daniel says as he washes the dishes in the sink and she sits at the table with another glass of juice, a slight shake still apparent in her hand.

"Okay, use the phone in the bedroom," she says. Then, starting to explain, "Daniel, I—"

"It's all right. It's no big deal."

"But I want to tell you."

"Okay."

"I want it—everything between us—to be perfect, untainted. I don't want you to be a part of what's going on in this family. Everyone's totally crazy, and I'm afraid if we—you and I . . . Then every time we made love it would come down on us again, it would come back. We would always carry this craziness around in us. I don't want you part of it."

"It's too late. . . ."

"I know!" She looks at him with demanding urgency, with a tightening grip so there is no refusing, her brown eyes wide and wild: "Just stay close to me, be here," the eyes of a visionary, adaptable to darkness, to other worlds.

Daniel goes to the master bedroom and sits on Calvin's unmade bed, on the side where Rae would have slept. He needs to call his friend Marty to ask him to take notes in history today. Might as well stay another day. At this moment he cannot imagine ever returning to college. He will not return.

Then, watching Lester drive past the window in his crumpled, sagging Dodge Coronet, he notices that Calvin and Rae's bedroom is a mess. Daniel wonders how long it has been since Rae slept here. Weeks? Months? The room is disheveled, almost ransacked. He looks around at the pictures of Rae's racehorses on the wall and a cluttered shelf of horse show trophies, and then the boxes of broken pots and obsidian scrapers and bone beads and a Kodacolor picture of her standing in an excavated pit house, holding up a pot.

Daniel looks outside across the withered alfalfa toward the mountains, south, toward the city and a vague new threat of emptiness like a river that has run strong in storm but now trickles, soon to run dry. He can hear Ruby and Lester moving about in the kitchen and he feels a nudging jealousy, then a needle of anger gouging the old wound of betrayal—though who had betrayed him never seemed clear. Shying from these thoughts, he quickly calls Marty, then hurries out of the bedroom and down the hallway back to the kitchen, Lester, and Ruby.

"Hey, Les," he says, and he senses they have not been talking.

Lester is quiet, half sitting against the counter, his long blond hair pulled back in a loose ponytail and his beard stringy and disheveled and thin except for the mustache and the sprouting clump on his chin. He has his spurs and chaps on and he looks very serious and Daniel believes Lester knows where Calvin left Rae.

"So I guess everybody's riding," Lester says.

"I want to go back on Mesa Reina," Ruby answers.

"There aren't gonna be any bulls up in there," Lester objects.

"I know that."

Lester nods, looks inquiringly at Daniel, who is unsure exactly where the fulcrum of this conversation rests, but he assumes it is with Ruby.

"I just want to ride around up there," Ruby is saying, now looking at Daniel, her feral eyes noisy with power yet opaque, the split gaze of double vision, and Lester expresses his discomfort over their wordless exchange by standing up from the counter and facing out the window.

"Ruby knows, Les," Daniel says, meaning the Indian-style burial.

"There's more to it, Daniel," Ruby says. Now she and Lester lock eyes, each measuring the other. "It's Mom's journals, okay? Look, I need to find them before Dad or Tomás does. They're out looking, huh, Lester?"

"Is it some legal thing?" Daniel asks.

"No. Well, partly."

"So what's the big secret?"

"Which one?" she retorts. Then: "I'm going to change clothes—I can't ride like this," she says, gesturing down at her white shoes and light pants. "I'll be right back." She holds out her hand like a stop sign to keep Daniel from following. He watches her quick-step down the path toward the bunkhouse.

After she's gone, Lester continues: "It's about the will, I suppose. Calvin's probably going to contest it, if it turns up."

"It's lost?"

"Well, nobody knows where it is. Rae either hid it or it burned up in the fire out at Turkey Springs. The lawyer doesn't seem to have a copy."

"Then how does anybody know what's in the will?"

"Tomás and I witnessed it. I guess she blurted out something to Calvin in a fight too, about him not being in her will. Anyhow, if nobody can find it—or suppose Calvin finds it and destroys it—then all Rae's property goes into probate and Calvin will keep the ranch that way."

"Didn't she give him anything?" Daniel asks. "Does Calvin still own any of the ranch?"

"Oh, yeah, well, the Forest Service lease back up in there." Lester nods toward the high mesas. "Not much. You could hardly call it pasture. Calvin figures if the will turns up but he has the journals, he'll have a case for contesting the will."

"So Calvin wants the journals to prove she was crazy. . . ."

"Of course—not that anyone needs to prove that. He thinks she went over the rainbow, you know? Living out there on Turkey Springs and creeping around the hills and hardly talking to anybody. Desert fever. It's all in those journals. At least, he could try to make a case that her mental state was paranoid or something, so she didn't know what she was doing when she rewrote the will. She was taking a lot of medication this fall."

"Have you read the journals?" Daniels presses.

"Rae confided in me, some." Lester faces back toward the window. "Ruby thinks I know where they are."

"Do you?"

Lester shrugs and he turns to look out the window across the ranch.

"How do you know Calvin hasn't found them yet?" Daniel asks.

"Cuz he's still looking. I went out there with them last night," he says, tipping his head to the southwest, toward the canyon where the Turkey Springs creek hits the river. "They took flashlights and kind of scraped around the foundation. They still don't know how it happened. The insurance company's gotta investigate. It was a strange night. Being out there last night was like being in a dream, somebody else's dream."

Ruby returns to the house in tight cowgirl jeans and a plaid shirt over a white tank top.

"I guess we should get started," Daniel suggests.

"You're going to ride your horse?" Lester asks, and he nods. "Who are you taking out, Ruby?"

"Oh—Boca, I suppose. It doesn't matter," and Lester's eyes wince at her tone, which is dismissive and distracted. She starts as if for the door, then turns and walks back to the center of the room and abruptly turns toward the table, folding her arms across her chest and tucking her chin and sniffling her nose.

"We don't have to go anywhere," Daniel says.

She shakes her head. "I know it." Poised for flight, Lester watches them, shifting his weight so he is infinitesimally farther away from Ruby.

"Maybe we should stay here," Daniel continues, uncertain where her thoughts have gone.

"Where did you all go last night?" Ruby asks, her voice aimed at Lester.

"I don't know what you think—"

"Yes, you do!" Ruby nearly shouts.

"You know we went to Turkey Springs," Lester answers.

"Did you find anything?"

"No."

"Don't you guys understand? Dad doesn't want to find anything. Not the journals. Not the will. Now that Mom's gone, nobody but me knows what Dad did to me, but it's all in those journals. So now he's almost in the clear. You can go out there as many times as you want, you can dig through the ashes of that house with a spoon, but you still won't know what Mom thought. That's why he put her up there. He won. But I know what happened, how Mom . . ."

—while sunlight rolls in rhythmic waves across her—

Lester tells Daniel with his eyebrows and a nod that he will wait outside.

"I still want to go," she says. "I'm going to find them first."

"Okay," Daniel answers. "Let's go."

7.

RUBY BEGAN TO SMOLDER with sensuality in high school, her face emerging in wild dark-eyed angles that incited uneasy, undeniable longings in Daniel on warm summer nights when the bats would dive and click above their heads as they sat around the fire pit that he had built behind the bunkhouse. He and Harvey would start laying branches on the flames as dusk fell, the sparks shooting upward in clusters like fizzing firecrackers, and Ruby was still young enough that Rae would let her come over only with stern warnings and a rigid curfew: she was still a girl, her hair long, long down her back, swaying as she moved with surprised leggy abruptness. Still a teenager himself, Daniel had started to think of her as available.

"I saw a coyote today, really close-up," she told him one night when the fire was so bright it blotted out all the stars. Harvey had gone home early so they sat alone, Ruby in a metal chair and Daniel leaning against a comfortable stump. "It was so astonishing," she continued, pronouncing "astonishing" with the particular clarity of one testing the effect of a newfound word, so Daniel gave her time to tell it, coyotes being too common to draw much interest on a ranch except as a target. She pointed her toe in its white sneaker toward the fire, then tapped it in the dust, acting suddenly embarrassed, as if she in this instant saw that he could be a man and she a woman, and perhaps even wondering whether to continue, so he prompted: "Where?"

"Oh, not too far past the irrigation pond, up Water Canyon. Mom had gone out that way. I told her I wanted to go when she went for her walk, but she went on without me. I guess she couldn't find me. So I looked for her footprints and I tracked her. I felt like an Indian." She shot him a pointed glance, measuring his interest in the story.

"Didja braid your hair?" he teased, nudging her toe with his own.

"No! But I walked really quiet." She laughed. "I could see where her hiking boots headed up this little arroyo in the canyon, so I followed them, but then I noticed there were dog tracks, and I knew our dogs were with Dad out on the flats, so I wondered what dog she was walking with. They seemed fresh. I mean, I don't really know what fresh tracks look like, but they seemed, you know, sharp. They had sharp edges." Ruby was wound up in the telling, getting breathless as she spoke and still checking his eyes in the flickering light. "And that arroyo gets deep. It's like ten feet on both sides and you feel like you're walking down the hallway of a castle where the roof caved in, because it's smooth and narrow and has all these sharp turns."

"Were you scared?"

"No. I knew Mom was up ahead of me, so I kept going. But then, you know, the sand turns into this hard rock, almost like cement, and I couldn't see her tracks anymore, but the dog tracks—I thought they were dog tracks—kept going, because I could see them in the sandy parts. But I couldn't see Mom's boots anymore. It's like, I don't know."

"What?"

"I . . . kept walking because those dog tracks kept going, and I was wondering where Mom had gone and when I looked up, something made me look up, and I saw it, this long pointy nose and stand-up ears. It had yellow eyes, I remember. It was straight above me, at the edge of the arroyo like ten feet above my head. We looked at each other. It was calm. I wasn't afraid. It seemed like a familiar thing. Then it vanished. It didn't turn away, or back up or spin around on its haunches. It just disappeared. Gone."

"Wow." Daniel watched Ruby watch the fire. In its red irregular light he could see her as she would look when she was twenty, when she was all grown up, with Rae's patrician features tempered by her own·sly gentleness, a deflecting of light into shadow.

She checked him again with her eyes, so round and trusting. "You think I'm a silly girl," she said with a detached adult huskiness so contrary to that open look.

"No. Then what happened?"

"I stood there for a second, thinking, like, did this really happen? And then I climbed up out of the arroyo, and there was Mom! That's the incredible thing. And I said, 'Did you see that coyote? He must have gone right past you!' She was sitting on a rock in the shade, like she'd been sitting there a while, and she shook her head. She said she liked to go out there to pray and meditate. I didn't know Mom prayed. She's not religious, like Dad is. The only time she ever goes to church is on a holiday, and she doesn't even wear a dress." Ruby was scowling at the flames and jiggling her foot.

"What was she praying for?" Daniel asked.

"I don't know. But we sat together for a while, and she asked me if I could be an animal, what it would be."

"A coyote," Daniel guessed.

"Of course!" Her smile flashed across the night. "She said that was a good choice. That's what she always wanted to be. Then when we got home she said she had a migraine and she hid in her room in the dark a couple days." After a few moments, Ruby stood. "I'd better go before Dad comes after me."

8.

CALVIN ALWAYS SAID RAE would bring home any stray she found, and true to form one hot June day she pulled up to the bunkhouse with Lester in the car, a tall, skinny hippie with blond hair halfway down his back. It was Daniel's second summer on the ranch. As Lester dragged his backpack and a battered guitar case out of the backseat of the car, Rae came to Daniel's door, introduced the two young men to each other, told Lester to come for dinner at the house at seven, and instructed Daniel to show him around the place.

Daniel took him into the room next door. Lester threw his pack onto the top bunk and said, "I am one tired motherfucker."

"Where'd you come from?" Daniel asked, leaning against the wall while Lester fell facedown on the bottom bed. Daniel had worked with other temporary hands before on the ranch so he was used to breaking the ice. At least this guy spoke English.

"Yesterday I was in Amarillo," he said. "Then I caught a ride all the way to Santa Fe. No air-conditioning, though. Then this lady—"

"Rae's her name—"

"—picked me up right outside of town there. What, there's an opera there or something?"

"Yeah, the Santa Fe Opera."

"She said you raise horses here."

"Yeah, they do."

"So you work here?"

"Yeah."

"Sounds cool."

"It's pretty cool."

"I'm just looking for a place to rack for a while."

Daniel took Lester down to the house for dinner around seven. They sat at the big table in the dining room with Harvey while from the kitchen Rae shuttled bowls of potatoes and peas, and big plates of sliced beef, everything steaming and good smelling, and Lester looked around the house nonchalantly while Daniel and Harvey talked about horses. Then Calvin came in after a day up in Colorado, stepping through the door and upon seeing Lester at the table politely walking over to introduce himself. Lester stood awkwardly. "I'm Lester Johnson. I guess I'm gonna work for you for a little while."

"Well, that's fine," Calvin said. "I'm glad to have you," but Daniel saw confusion unsettling Calvin's eyes, which were restless and leapt around Lester's face, then to Daniel, to Harvey. "I better go wash up," Calvin concluded as Rae returned.

"Go call Ruby," she told him, "and hurry. We're all ready."

Ruby came from her room, which had its own entrance across a small courtyard. She demurely took her seat across from Daniel.

"Lester, this is my daughter, Maryanne," Rae said as everyone sat down. "We all call her Ruby," and as Ruby said "hi" to him Rae stared at her a moment in a double take as Daniel too saw the inexpertly applied eye shadow and mascara.

"Young lady, did I say you could wear makeup?" Rae asked, her voice glacially quiet.

"Oh, Mom!" And Ruby looked to Daniel for support, then Harvey, who was too young to assess the politics of this disagreement.

"I think it looks good," Daniel offered.

"You stay out of this!" Rae snapped. "Now go wash it off," and while Ruby shoved her chair back from the table and flung her napkin down, Daniel saw Calvin standing in the dining room doorway, taking it all in, but when Ruby squeezed past him he turned and followed her out the door to the courtyard and her room.

"Harvey, pass Lester the beef, if you would, and let's get started," Rae said, raising her glass and taking a long draught of water: "It was a hot day today. . . ."

Calvin returned alone.

When they finished eating, Ruby still hadn't left her room, and Daniel helped Harvey clear the table and do dishes, then went with Calvin to the corral to doctor a sick foal.

The filly—Wheeler, they called her, because she spun so nicely on her hocks—had an eye infection, and Daniel pinned the foal against a wooden fence corner while Calvin squeezed ointment from a tube under her upper eyelid, and Wheeler would leap in Daniel's arms, standing almost straight up in her blind rush to get away while her mother pawed and snorted at the post where she was tied. Then when Calvin was done they petted the filly and led her around until she quieted down, and Daniel turned her loose first, then the mare.

As they watched the pair canter back to their place along the feed trough where the other horses milled about, waiting for their hay, Calvin said, "Little Wheeler's going to be a cutting horse. You can tell by the way she moves, and the way she turns so low down to the ground. And she watches the cattle. She lowers her head to watch them. She's attentive." Daniel followed Calvin through the fence to the truck. "I think I'll let Harvey break her—by then Harvey will be old enough. And he'll make a good horse trainer. You know, I like to look at the foals and guess what they'll be like. When Tripper was young, you could see he was never going to be an athlete. Some horses you can't tell, of course, until they get a little older."

They climbed into the truck. Calvin drove around the corral, stopping the truck by the haystack in the barn. Daniel got out, grabbed a pitchfork, and started throwing hay into the manger for the horses, who shoved each other and pinned their ears as they took their places in line, then settled down as each was fed. When they were all quietly chewing, nose down in the sweet-smelling alfalfa and grass, Daniel stood beside Calvin, whose satisfaction with the herd was palpable, leaning on the handle of his pitchfork, resting his chin on its butt end, looking at little Wheeler.

"Sometimes I dream about setting one like this loose with the mustangs, letting it run wild," Calvin said. "It would be such a great horse, so beautiful it made your heart ache, and I would take it up on top of the mesas and turn it loose. It would be such a horse you had to turn it loose, because you couldn't do anything else with it—it would have too much pride, and it would kill itself when you tried to break it. It wouldn't be right to lay a hand on it. Maybe it never is."

The men stood together and looked at the horses munching their hay from the wooden crib, its boards worn to a smooth, silvery patina by horses rubbing as they ate, by the rain and sun. Calvin went quiet again and Daniel was content to lean on the top board of the corral and feel the peacefulness of the big animals. Then Calvin spoke up again. "It's a crazy, beautiful idea, thinking about watching that filly tear off, wild. Wild. Never broke, never a man on her back. . . . I guess I got a little girl like that, instead."

Calvin set down his pitchfork and opened the gate to the corral, giving the older mares a wide berth as he walked behind them, then sidling up beside the filly, who continued chewing warily, watching him with white-rimmed eyes, her ears flicking in agitation. Calvin laid a hand on her rump and she flinched and stepped away but she didn't kick. "Horses never lie," he said. He ran his hand along her fuzzy back and walked up to her head, scratching her neck and talking low. In a minute the horse forgot him and went back to eating. "I could do anything with her now."

He stepped out of the corral through the boards. "Keeping horses seems so natural," Calvin said. "That's why I've stayed in ranching, even though we never made much money at it, especially now'days. But having the animals around, especially the horses, makes it all worthwhile. Sometimes I wonder if the horses are happy, though. I said that to my own father once, and he told me not to bother with such foolish thoughts. He was a stern man, God-fearing. He didn't concern himself with such trifles. He hated sentimentality. He believed in reason, the power of the mind to understand, to reason through any problem. 'That's the tool God gave us to hold dominion over the world and the animals,' he would say. My lord, how he and Rae would argue. He liked her, though. That's a fact. He never knew a woman like her. Who did?"

Calvin kept talking as they headed for the truck to drive out and fill salt boxes for the cattle on pasture. "In the fall, we would turn most of the horses out for winter and keep a few in the barn. As a boy, it was my favorite thing, riding out with my father, driving a herd of twenty horses across the creek to the flats, and watching them run. They knew they were free for five months. And my horse would prance and rear up, doing all he could to go with them. It was always a sad moment when we turned back. Our mounts would call to the herd all the way home. Being around animals is good for the soul. I believe that. But it's sad that we can't let them live the way God intended. We left the Garden, I suppose, and brought them along with us to remind us what we gave up when we lost our innocence. And we can't go back."

After dinner, Rae came over to the bunkhouse, a rare event, in Daniel's experience. He and Les were sitting on the porch, their chairs tilted back to the wall and their feet on the posts that held up the roof.

"Well, boys, you look comfortable," she said, smiling as she approached. She wore silver bracelets heavy on her wrists and had pulled back her long hair into a tight bun. She looked pretty and young—still in her mid-thirties then—and Daniel realized he had never thought of her that way: always as a mother, never as a woman. "Are you feeling settled in, Lester?" she asked, stopping by one of the posts.

"Oh, yeah. It still feels all-new."

"As I've often told Daniel," and she nodded at him, "consider this your home for as long as you're here. Calvin and I believe in old-time hospitality. And of course we expect you to respect it as if it were your own home."

"Well, thanks a lot," Lester said, still tipping back in his chair and his eyes unblinking on her face. "I figure I'll move on in another week or so." All Daniel had learned so far was that Lester had spent a tour in Nam with an artillery unit. That was a year ago.

"Stay as long as you like. I need some muscle at the dig, and Daniel here is pretty well tied up with fieldwork."

"Right on," Lester said, his eyes leaping away across the flats toward the river and the deep-shadowed canyons to the southwest.

"Well, good night, boys," she said, smiling again, then striding quickly away, an athletic spring to her steps. Daniel saw Lester's eyes move off the landscape to watch Rae go.

Later, after all the lights on the ranch were out, Daniel heard a soft rap on his screen and Ruby's voice saying, "Daniel? Are you awake?" He said yeah and she came in through the darkness and found his desk chair. Sitting down, she said, "I felt like I needed somebody to talk to." She was quiet for a minute and he fumbled for the light, but she said, "Leave it dark, okay?" and he realized this act of defiance against her parents had its limits and all she would say was that Calvin had been keeping her up.

Then she sat quiet a few moments in the dark. He waited her out, until she said in a light tone that seemed carefully compensating for the tension of her previous silence, "Do you get along with your parents?"

"Oh, yeah, I suppose. Like anybody, we've had disagreements. . . . I remember when I was fourteen, we had this huge, I mean huge fight, because I wanted a motorcycle, and they wouldn't let me, and I went out and got an old Honda 125 anyway. I spent my lawn-mowing money."

"What happened?"

"They grounded me for a month. Then my friend Brad Hale got us in a car wreck. After that, my parents sent me up here to work. They figured Calvin would straighten me out. That was the first summer I worked here."

"I remember." She was quiet again, then said, "Why did she have to embarrass me in front of everyone? It's like I don't have any feelings."

"I know it. . . ."

"You see it too? It's not just me? I'm not being paranoid?"

"No. She's a little hard on you."

"You'd think wearing a little eye makeup was a sin, the way she acted. I think she doesn't want me to grow up—" Another pause filled the dark and he could hear her breathing across the room. "Did you like the way it looked?" her voice small as a child's.

"Yes."

"Really?"

"Oh, yeah," he says.

"I guess Dad did too."

"What do you mean?"

"Never mind. Thanks, Daniel. You're so sweet," and she slipped through the screen door into the night, leaving him awake another hour in a sweaty puddle.

9.

RUBY SITS IN THE MIDDLE between Lester and Daniel for the drive
to the barn. Lester drives slowly, the car creaky on the uneven
road and smelling strongly of hot oil. When they pull alongside
the corrals, Tomás is already mounted inside the barn, while
Calvin tightens the girth of his saddle, his horse squirming
away. Harvey stands beside his own horse, waiting. Daniel lets
Ruby lead into the barn, where all the saddles are lined up on
a long beam that serves as saddle rack. Lester stands just inside
the big doorway and leans against the wall.

"We caught Boca for you," Calvin says to Ruby as he
gathers his reins to mount. "She's tied up in the alley." He swings
up into the saddle and steps his horse alongside her. "How
are you, honey?" he asks softly, so Daniel can barely make out
the words.

"I'm all right," she says, but she steps back slightly, out of
range of further questions, and looks down the aisle between
corrals where her horse is tied.

"Why don't you three ride up the creek and look for tracks,"
Calvin suggests. "The three of us are going to head across the
flats and ride the river."

"We're going up onto Mesa Reina, up the canyon," she says.

"You won't find any bulls up there," he says with a little laugh and a glance at Tomás.

"That's where we're going," Ruby answers, and she walks past him into the alley, unties Boca, and leads the mare back into the barn for saddling.

"I guess I better go get my horse," Daniel says to no one in particular, but Lester says, "Why don't you throw your tack in my car and drive down there? We'll meet you on the road," and Ruby doesn't even look up from grooming Boca as he hauls his old saddle out of the tack room and carries it to the car, then comes back for a halter and bridle.

Harvey walks his horse over toward the car, and Daniel waits for him before driving off. Lester has grabbed a rope and headed off to catch a horse from the corral.

"What's up?" Daniel asks lightly.

"I feel like I oughta tell you. . . ."

"What?"

"Last night we drove out to the Turkey Springs house—or what's left of it. Just a pile of ashes."

"I know it."

"Even the walls caved in, it got so hot. Me and Dad, and Lester and Tomás. We didn't want Ruby to know."

"Why?"

"They wanted to find Mom's journals first. Tomás said— he said it would be too hard for her. . . ."

"Bullshit," Daniel says, and he remembers Ruby at the burial site, her hair like a hood about her face, her eyes commanding him to be still, to wait with her for—

Harvey slaps his reins idly against his palm. "Well, we went out there because Tomás wanted to see—"

"Let's go, Harv!" Calvin calls then. "Let's ride."

"Anyhow," Harvey says, swinging aboard, turning his horse

toward the others. "It doesn't matter. There wasn't anything to see. See you at lunch," he calls to Daniel as he trots away.

Daniel drives down to the pasture again to catch his horse. The gelding is finishing his pile of hay. Daniel halters him and quickly brushes off his back, then throws the blanket and saddle on, puts the bit in his mouth, and leads the horse quickly out of the field onto the road. He feels a new urgency, there is no time to be lost, no time—even letting Turk lope the road without warming him up, in a steady canter rounding the curve where the hills below Mesa Reina jut onto the plain, then pulling the horse up as he approaches Ruby and Lester, who have started up the road. In silence they ride past the fields, then the house, and along the upper pastures to the little irrigation reservoir and the grave site. Still the day grows warmer, and Daniel can't resist the exultation of being horseback in this country again while the cliffs on three sides soar into the cobalt sky and the deep shadows of autumn and the new silence from the quiet beyond and Ruby riding beside him beautiful despite possession—or because of it—the quiet beyond leaking into his thoughts and mixing with the sunlight on her hair and her face, mixing with the colors of sandstone cliffs, orange, yellow, red, white-capped like teeth at the southeastern point of Mesa Reina, a place as barren and blasted and nourishing as the moon, where footsteps echo hollow and birds sometimes hover outside of time where the unceasing updraft sweeps over the lip of the mesa and holds them aloft without effort.

So he reins Turk closer and she looks at him a moment it seems without recognizing him, then her eyes resolve this world, their opacity yields to a more watery softness.

"What are you thinking?" he asks.

"Oh. All of it. I dreamed all night, you know. They were so vivid. In living color—living."

"About Rae?"

She nods. "And Dad . . . and you."

—charmed out of time—

"I dreamed about her too."

"You did?"

"Yeah. I don't remember it very well," he lies.

"There are some things I can't talk about yet," she says. Ahead, Lester jogs his horse.

A while later, as they follow the trail into the wooded canyon, along the stream, which is full and brown and wide with snow-melt, she says, "Mom wrote in her diary every day, you know, and sketched sometimes too." She looks at Daniel. "Every day. It was incredible. Sometimes she would read to me from it, about Alaska and the dig up there—"

—where she would cradle those mysterious ivory carvings in her hand, images tiny and transformational, through her vision the man becoming the seal becoming the water becoming the ivory in her hand—

"—or her thoughts on a day. But she always read old stuff to me, nothing recent, nothing about me or Dad or Harvey, but I knew she wrote about that too. She kept it—the current volume and the old ones—in a metal strongbox, and she always kept it with her, wherever she was." Again Ruby's eyes go wide with that wild urgency. "Don't you see what they were looking for last night? The journal. He wants to read it, he wants to know everything she wrote! He'll use them against her and then he'll probably burn them!" She shakes her head as if she could shake away a memory. "He knows I'll use them against him."

"Harvey said they didn't find anything," Daniel says quietly and, he hopes, supportively, afraid of her mood.

"They won't," she murmurs after the horses' hooves have drummed out a minute on the damp sandy trail through cottonwoods and Gambel oak and the canyon walls grow narrow, closing in on them like possession—

She nods toward Lester and says, "And he knows where they are."

"How?"

—or drums beating—

But she won't answer.

"Do you?" he persists.

"Oh, yes. I have an idea."

—images of shaman who like seals would dive to the ocean floor, like seals diving under the ice and wrestling with good and evil spirits, yet returning—

"Are they up in here?" Daniel asks.

"No," Ruby says, still watching Lester. "But I want to find Mom first. Or the burial, anyhow. How else can I be sure any of this is real?"

The trail squeezes in, and they must ride single file, Lester still leading far out in front, letting his horse jog where it isn't too rocky. Daniel lets Ruby ride ahead of him, though his horse walks faster and often crowds Boca, but he enjoys riding behind Ruby, enjoys the rhythmic rise and fall of her hips from the saddle when she trots, and in a light moment he has to say: "You look pretty good on a horse," and she twists to look back at him with a smile, even slightly embarrassed, yet she retorts, "I always was known for my riding form." Then at a wide spot where the trail crosses the creek, she reins to the side and lets Daniel come along beside her.

"Will you stay over tonight?" she asks. Lester has forded the stream and is waiting on the other side, out of earshot. "We could try again."

"I've got to go back sometime," he says, breezing past an offer that seems halfhearted.

"Why?"

"Cuz."

She looks down at her hands on the saddle horn, while on the far bank Lester's horse grows restless, and finally he turns him up the trail and disappears into the trees, climbing a steep hill out of sight.

"Why don't you come down with me?" he suggests. "You can stay as long as you want. You can stay forever. . . ."

"No." She sighs. "I've got to be here. There's too much going on right now," she says. "It's like I said earlier, so stirred up, I don't know what I think, what I want. But you're part of it all, somehow. You have to be here. I feel like you're the only steady thing I've got right now: at least that's become clear. Why have we wasted so much time?"

"I don't know. We haven't. You can't waste it."

"Yes, you can."

10.

ONE DAY IN LATE SPRING, when Ruby was a senior in high school and Daniel was working on the ranch year-round, Calvin asked him to drive Rae with the dump truck into town and pick up a load of sweet feed and salt blocks, then swing by and get Ruby from school. He brought the truck around to the front of the house and Rae climbed up the step into the cab, her long silver earrings dangling and her dark hair in a long ropy braid. "Thank you for doing this," she said. "I can't drive this big thing," which Daniel knew to be untrue, but she hated to be seen driving a two-ton dump truck around town. They didn't speak as they bounced down the ranch road, climbed the hill onto the plateau of the home pasture, and descended to the cattle guard by the highway. Rae had been rummaging through her purse, then she burst out: "Stop! Oh, fiddle. I think I left my wallet in the house. Could you turn back, please?"

So Daniel did a big circle on the highway and steamed up the hill back to the house, and Rae jumped out and ran in the front door, then came right out again.

"Well," she said. "I guess I had it with me all along," smiling and softened by embarrassment. "Calvin says I'm neurotic, but he doesn't really know what that means."

When they drove past the village on the bluff across the river from the highway, Daniel told her about the petroglyphs he had found up behind the house he was sharing with Lester. He described their shape, drawing in the air with his finger, and talked about how they looked pecked, not carved, into the basalt and were yellowy with age. He went on to tell how he had followed a coyote to them, and it seemed every rock within a quarter acre of that boulder field had a picture on it.

"I almost felt like I was being watched," he admitted.

"Yes," she said. "I know something of that feeling. Could you take me to them?"

"Sure," he said.

"Studying rock art is so imprecise," she said, as if beginning a lecture. "They're impossible to date. Even if you find other material culture remains around the site, you don't know if you're dealing with intrusion or contemporary materials. It's so inexact, but so fascinating. Partly it's that mystery and how it opens the door to subjective interpretation." She fell quiet again and looked across the river to the mesas. "Where were you, exactly?"

"Above the river, there, to the west of Six Mile Creek."

"Can you find them again? Did you ever go back?"

"No, I didn't. I think I can."

"Sometimes," she said, "I think this desert swallows things up. It absorbs them. The landscape has a rhythm; it's repetitive in some way. I spent a few summers by the ocean, you know, visiting my grandparents in North Carolina. Sometimes out on the water you get the same feeling, that you know generally where you are, but not exactly. That's unsettling, somehow, I think. It's morally unsettling. It creates an ambiguity. I've been here all of my life, off and on, and there are times when it still looks completely strange to me."

They reached a steep hill where the truck, with its accelerator floored, was too loud for conversation, but at the top, Daniel said, "You hear people say that all great religions were founded in the desert."

Rae turned to look at him. He could feel those eyes hot against his skin: "What is a 'great religion'?"

He smiled despite the irritation he heard in her voice, but abruptly her mood shifted again, and she preempted his answer: "I guess that leaves us Protestants out in the cold," she added. "Don't tell Calvin, he'll be very disappointed." Then after a few more miles had rolled by: "I worry about Ruby growing up here, though. It's not a good place for a girl." Daniel senses but doesn't grasp an ominous implication in her tone. "She needs to get away, to see more of the world than this ranch and Las Colinas."

"She seems happy. . . ."

"Oh, she's happy anywhere, as long as there are boys around," and Daniel noted the disapproval in her voice. "But someday she'll have to learn that those looks won't get her everything she wants. She's already learning it gets her attention she doesn't want. She needs to be prepared, she needs skills. She can't charm her way through life."

"I think you sell her short," Daniel dared to say, and again felt her gaze, but when he met her eyes he found them appraising, not scolding.

"Do you?"

"Ruby is . . ." He couldn't think of the right word.

"Oh, you're charmed too," she said dismissively. "Well . . . She's just a girl yet, Daniel. I wish everyone could remember that." Daniel felt embarrassed, apprehended, even guilty for the evenings spent talking with Ruby and playing around on the porch of the bunkhouse or down on the flat rocks by the lake, innocent of action but not of thought, guilty for his infatuation with her growing sensuality, for his dreams.

He sat in the truck outside the school while Rae wrote in her journal and frequently gazed out the window with the pen caught between her teeth. Not wishing to disturb her thoughts and uncomfortable with the silence, he stepped down to the sidewalk and leaned against the fender, watching traffic roll by and wondering in which classroom Ruby was sitting, counting the minutes until that final bell: then it rang and kids crowded down the walkway that bisected the front lawn and there was Ruby, coming alone with an armload of books hugged to her chest, her face narrowed in self-involved concentration, then she spotted Daniel and smiled and stopped beside him, shifting the books into the crook of one arm so she could brush her hair from her face.

"Hey, gorgeous," he called.

"Hi," she said. "What are you doing here? Pickin' up high school girls? Don't you wish!"

"Wanna take a little ride, sweetheart?"

"Oh, I don't know." She looked him over as if sizing him up, going along with the game. "It's going to be kind of hard with my mother in the truck, isn't it?"

"We'll ditch her at Lucifer's Grill. She can have a few drinks . . ." and they both laughed because Rae was a teetotaler. "Let's go," he said, and she climbed in the driver's side ahead of him, settling into the seat between Daniel and her mother. "Hi, Mom."

—she would blow him apart, then gather the pieces together—

She leaned lightly against him for the drive home, and his arm brushed her bare legs every time he shifted the heavy truck gears, but Rae was preoccupied and finally, when they were on the highway after crossing the river by the pueblo, she said, "There's a letter from Stanford waiting for you, Ruby," and Daniel could see a conspiratorial excitement in Rae's eyes when he looked across at the two women.

"No kidding?" Ruby said flatly.

"You've been waiting for that one."

"No—you've been waiting for it. Did you read it?"

"No, it's addressed to you. I never read other people's mail. I thought you'd be pleased. I'm sure they've accepted you."

"I don't want to go. . . ."

In Rae's silence and Ruby's sudden stiffness at his side Daniel felt the struggle between wills begin, the battle lines drawn, an old war engaging on a new front: college. "Ruby . . ."

"Mom!"

"We'll talk about this when we get home," Rae said.

"Let's talk about it now. Daniel doesn't mind."

"C'mon, Ruby," he protested.

"Who's side are you on?" she countered.

"Uhhh . . ."

"Oh, thanks a lot," Ruby said, but Rae was back to looking out the window and would say no more.

When they reached the ranch, Daniel dropped the two women at the house, Rae exiting quickly while Ruby took a moment to gather her books, and as she slid across the seat to get out he said, "Ruby?"

"What?"

"I'm always on your side."

Then she smiled gaily, as if ending a performance: "I know," her teeth flashing like stars. "You I'm not worried about. Bye!"

The next night Ruby drove over to the house he was renting in the village with Lester. They'd both moved off the ranch in March.

"Am I crazy not going to college?" she called out coming

through the back door as the sun died in the west, a pure orange April sunset hinting of the summer to follow. "Dad wants me to stay, but that's reason enough to go. I don't think I'm cut out for college. I need more action. Then Mom makes it sound like I'm a bad person if I don't, like I'll never be anything."

Ruby hadn't phoned ahead and he wasn't expecting her. Having her alone in his kitchen thrilled him, made her seem an available adult. "But I don't even know what I want to be," she finished as he gave her a chair at the kitchen table. He sat up on the counter by the sink, finishing off a beer. "Listen, Ruby, all I can really tell you—and Rae would probably strike me down for saying this—is that it's your decision. College doesn't work out for everybody, sure, but a lot of people get a kick out of it too."

"Why did you drop out?"

"I'm going back."

"When?"

"Probably next fall."

"Why?"

"I feel I need to finish. I started it, I ought to finish it," he answered.

"So you'll be gone next year," she said.

"I can't work for your dad forever."

"You've always been so decent to me, you and Lester." She looked down at the floor and one-fingered a lock of hair behind her ear. "Daniel?"

"Yeah?"

She didn't say anything for a minute, then she looked up at him and he saw how the last of that pubescent fleshiness had dropped from her cheekbones and she was no longer merely pretty, she was breathtaking, dark-eyed and dark-skinned from an obscure ancestor but with her mother's cut-glass cheekbones and thin elegant nose—and a keening look drew her brow together, the struggle of an emotion toward words. She held his gaze, her eyes like a woman's steady with the wisdom of disappointment. Then her eyes dropped from his and he would later guess what she might have said, but he would never know because he had not dared to ask so soon after Rae's "she's just a girl" speech.

In lesser misdemeanor he fetched a cold bottle from the refrigerator and said, "Jesus, don't ever tell your mother how many beers I've bought for you—here I am, corrupting a minor." Ruby was by then recovered from whatever melancholy had possessed her, so that when she took the bottle she retorted smartly, "Shit, Dan, I was born corrupt," as she twisted off the cap with a towel protecting her hand. "You know what Dad says: I was born old. He says I never was a little kid. It suits him to think that. . . . Mom thinks I have an 'old soul.' But I really don't know what that means."

"I guess it means I'm not the first to corrupt you," he said, but the way she dropped her eyes and grew still made him regret his words. "At least, I can give you a beer."

"I guess so." She took a swig and set the bottle down on the table in front of her, slowly rotating it in her outstretched hands.

"Could I take you out to dinner for a graduation present?" he asked then, his words thick with a sudden nervousness.

She showed no surprise when she answered. "Of course. Yes—"

"In a few weeks, when summer is really here. After you graduate. When we can sit outside at Chimayó."

"Just you and me?"

"Is that okay?"

"Oh, yes—"

11.

"LET'S CAMP TONIGHT," he tells Ruby, while his horse rubs its sweaty face against Boca's shoulder. "Let's drive out to Willard's. It won't be so cold tonight," and then the next day disappear up the canyon into the mountains, never looking back, going deeper and deeper, spiraling centerward, a successive shedding of layers, a gradual peeling away, and a settling—

"No, not tonight," she says now. "We'll camp some other night. I need to stay close by. There's a current running through us all right now," Ruby is saying. "It's building and building, and it gets hotter and hotter and hotter. It's like electricity flowing. And I think: what if we all catch fire?"

—into an older rhythm and the satisfaction of ancient hungers, as before the first plucking—

She urges Boca into the stream, then Daniel follows on Turk.

The trail climbs steeply, winding among tall ponderosa, then breaking out on the hillside halfway up the canyon and paralleling the stream. From their newly gained elevation they can see out the mouth of the canyon all the way to the valley past the fields and buildings of the ranch in the foreground.

Ahead, Lester scrambles his horse up the last steep pitch that skirts the canyon's box. He slips from view around a rock face, then emerges a few minutes later in the meadow above, out of the canyon. Ruby holds her horse back so Daniel can lead on the ascent, and Turk gallops up the rocky trail, slowing his pace only when big rocks interrupt the path or to gather himself for a leap up an especially steep spot. When Daniel reaches the top, Lester is dismounted waiting for him, and together they wait for Ruby, out of sight below.

"Where do you think we're going?" Lester asks.

"I have no idea," Daniel answers.

"Does she?"

"I have no idea," he repeats. "Should I ask?"

"No—it's not really important, is it? I mean, Rae is dead. . . ."

Lester's face, so thin it's gaunt, is prematurely aged, and people on first meeting him often wonder if he is a cleric—say, a fallen-away Lutheran minister, a Norse monk. His eyes are deep blue and deeply set, and now they regard Daniel from a vault of introspection, a self-awareness so attuned to inner thoughts that even simple eye contact seems the intrusion into a private world. "Someday," Daniel says as if he's joking, "I'm going to ask you what's really going on around here."

"Someday," Lester says, matching his tone but his eyes still as abstract as the sky above them, "I'll know." Ruby appears then, her horse moving slowly around the rock outcrop that guards the top of the trail. "Ask her. It's Ruby's gig. She's running the show."

When Ruby reaches them, she says, "Boca is such a wuss. She can't keep up."

"That's all right," Daniel says. "We'll wait."

Ruby dismounts and checks the saddle girth, pulling it

tighter another notch. Then she turns and looks east, up to the rim, the right arm of Mesa Reina. The trail heads north. "Let's go up that way," she says, still looking to the rim.

"There's no way to get up there," Lester protests. "The last fifty feet are practically straight up."

"No," she says. "There's a way around back. I rode up there with Mom once. I'll show you—" Then when Lester still looks doubtful, she adds, "You don't have to come, but I want to do it."

"All right," Lester says, and Daniel already is on his horse. "You lead, girl."

For half an hour they ride behind Ruby. At first the going is easy. She crosses the sandy wash that flows to the south and terminates at the top of the canyon's box from which they have emerged; she leads them across a grassy meadow then up a graveled pitch, and soon the horses are stepping over deadfall trees and scrambling on the steep, loose rock. The slope is banded by strata of sandstone, each layer the compressed legacy of a million years undersea, and Daniel thinks Rae would have walked each stratum, "checking the fossil record," her eyes always scanning for some fresh window into the deep past.

Soon Turk is lathered under his breast collar and they stop the horses to let them blow and no one speaks. Then Ruby turns Boca again up the slope, standing in the saddle to get her weight forward, reining the mare around an ensnaring cluster of branches and loose rocks, winding her way higher and higher above the two men, who sit and watch her go, the sun a bright pinpoint of heat on their faces and the air cold on their backs. She cuts laterally across the slope a while, then again turns the mare into the hill, and from where they stand it seems she is going vertically straight up the mesa. After perhaps ten minutes she stops and turns Boca sideways to the slope, directly below the rim rock, which rears above her in vertical slabs like tombstones. She regards Daniel and Lester, her horse's legs quivering from the strain, the mare shaking her head and blowing several times.

"Are you stuck?" Daniel calls to her, for it seems she has nowhere to go but back down. "No!" she calls back. "It's right through here! Are you coming?"

Daniel looks at Lester, who looks at him and says, "After you," so he points Turk up the hill and follows Boca's tracks. His horse is strong and takes the slope in lunging jumps. Daniel hangs on to a fistful of mane and stands, leaning far over Turk's shoulder and talking the horse on. When he reaches Ruby she moves her horse across the slope below the rim, and they hear Lester's horse now crashing his way uphill.

"Look," Ruby says, and Daniel follows the direction of her pointing finger to a narrow passageway leading up over the top between two huge sandstone boulders. "See?" she says as the horses walk the easy path through the rim. Leaning back in the saddle she tells him, "Mom said this was an old Indian trail. There's a ruin up here. They used this trail to go down into the canyon for water. It's the quickest way . . ." and they are on top of Mesa Reina's eastern arm.

"I didn't know there were any ruins up here," Daniel says.

"No, Mom never told anybody."

The river basin spreads out below them, with the broad grassy plains in the foreground, the mountains beyond blue and shadowy and broad as the southern horizon, with traces of snow on the peaks of Tecolote and Las Animas. Behind Daniel to the west, the divided ridge of Mesa Reina converges with its western arm and slopes northward to Cebolla Peak, a forest of pines and, higher, aspens and fir sweeping up to the conical summit. Far in the east and still shadowed by morning are the bald peaks and a haze lifting from the river, which is hidden by mesas in the middle distance.

"Jesus," Daniel says, "this place is too much."

But Ruby isn't listening. Her eyes have gone away again, as if all the gaping space around them had sucked out her soul and into the emptiness her visions poured, an obliterating flood such as had visited Noah, a flood of dreams, compressing like the ancient sea, each vision opening into another layer of awareness: this was how Rae saw the desert, he thinks, layer upon layer of awareness, spirit on spirit, an abyss of stratified consciousness, a clamoring of spirits, the unintelligible collective utterances and that brooding power seeping upward like water, soaking first the feet, then drawn into the body and mixing with the blood, dreams becoming watery like melted sandstone and dangerous, like sandstone her dreams melting into the deep past and the soul plunging as down an unending river rapids—she is a whirlpool tugging at him, urging him to dive under with her, to become like seals—

Her eyes catch him and hold him, her eyes recumbent, her face flushed, her mouth open, even her neck flushed red. Her tongue flicks across her teeth and she almost smiles at him, then her face collapses upon itself, her jaw sags, her eyes fill, she says, "Don't go away . . . please," as Lester rides up and pulls his horse to a stop above them as distant and dispassionate as galaxies.

12.

THE NIGHT OF THEIR DATE, Daniel was hurrying around the house getting dressed. Lester said, "Jailbait, man. Remember, sixteen'll get you twenty."

"She's almost eighteen, Les." A fear of consequence, of punishment, had always stayed his hand—but Ruby as a consenting adult opened up the possibilities.

"Seventeen is still statutory in this state."

"You want to go to hell? Screw you, anyhow."

"I'm just razzin' you, man, take it easy."

"You're just jealous."

Lester shrugged and went to sit in the living room. "You think Albert is gettin' any?" Albert was Ruby's current boyfriend, one of the school's star athletes who had a job in his father's auto parts store. "You think he gets it from her?"

"Probably, how the hell should I know? I'm taking her out to dinner, for chrissake. I consider her a good friend. It's mutual."

"It's mutual, all right, but you're scared to death of her mother," Lester pressed. "Ruby's got you, man. It's like malaria—it keeps coming back in relapses and you never really get rid of it."

Daniel was at the door and he turned to Lester as he stepped out. "Does that mean I have your permission?"

"By all means, my boy."

"Don't wait up . . ."

But when he arrived at the house and Rae let him in, Ruby wasn't ready, so he sat at the kitchen table as Calvin and Harvey finished their meal and Rae wasn't speaking to him. While he waited, he talked with Calvin about cutting the weeds in the orchard grass before they went to seed, and then Ruby appeared in a summery dress that bared her shoulders and her back and his knees felt a little unsteady as he rose from the chair at the table and even Harvey said, "Whoa! Now that's what I call pretty," and Calvin looked her up and down a moment too long but Rae was silent in the kitchen.

"I'm ready," Ruby said, and she spun so Daniel could admire her, smiling and not flustered as he watched.

"Let's go," he said.

"Okay, let me say bye to Mom," and Ruby stepped past to the kitchen, touching him as she went by. "I'm leaving, Mom," he heard her say, then Rae said something he didn't catch and Ruby said, "I will!" and she returned to Daniel, grabbing his hand and pulling him to the door, Daniel calling behind him, "See you all later," and then they were outside.

"Is Rae upset?" he asked when they were in the truck.

"Oh—it's nothing. We had a little talk about 'older men' earlier today. It's so fucking ironic—like I don't know. She wishes I was still a child," and he smelled her hair as she flipped it over her shoulders and the perfume she was wearing and he wanted to make some ultimate declaration to her and then all that skin hot every inch against him. "It's okay," Ruby concluded. "Thanks again for taking me. I've been looking forward to this."

"Me too," he said, and he drove her the forty miles to the restaurant, feeling strangely shy around her despite their years of friendship, but Ruby talked freely, a light patter of conversation at once breezy and intimate, so the miles rolled by and he felt intoxicated and detached, watching himself drive and Ruby sitting beside him, her hand sometimes alighting on his arm as if grounding her words in the contact of flesh to flesh.

"What does Albert think about you going out with me on a Friday night?" he asked after they had been seated up on the second-level terrace behind the restaurant. The waitress had lit the little candle in the center of the table and Daniel ordered two margaritas.

"Albert . . ." she said elliptically. "Albert's sweet, and he's kind of fun, that's all."

"You've been going out with him for a year."

"Well—sometimes there are people you spend time with just because they're there, you know? Some kind of security, or they're the answer to a question you didn't know you asked. It helps me with other guys to have him around. It sounds cold-blooded, I suppose, and it's really not—I don't think. He knows I'll be gone next fall, one way or another. I have to get away. You don't know what this family's really like."

"Everybody thinks that about their family," Daniel suggested, sensing she had more to say and wanting to steer her away from any revelation that might require him to confront— who? Calvin?

"No," she said, "not like this. Someday I'll tell you. Anyhow, there's got to be something better out there for me— and Albert's not part of that—something I'll do, something I'm supposed to do—"

"A mission."

"A mission," she agreed. "Not like Dad did in Alaska, not for the church, but for—I don't know. When I was little, I thought I was weird. It seemed like I was different from all the other little girls. I think Mom was part of it, because she was different. . . . I sometimes have dreams that come true," and she checked his face for a reaction. "I really do."

"I believe you."

"And then Mom told me once that she did too, that she actually dreamed where she would find the Turkey Springs pueblo, then she went out and found it."

Daniel nodded and the waitress brought them their drinks, not even questioning Ruby's age. Daniel picked up his glass and held it across the table to her for a toast: "To your dreams, then," he said, not meaning hopes and aspirations but—

—visions—

—those strange premonitions and she clinked glasses with him and kept her eyes on his while she drank and it was somehow erotic, those eyes so heavy-lidded slipping over the rim of the salty-lipped glass.

"I dream about you sometimes," she went on, energized, twisting slightly in her seat for this new foray.

"Oh, yeah?"

"Yeah," she confirmed, all woman now, her voice deep in her throat and she looked at him slightly sideways, peering from the corner of her eye. "Sometimes you're working with Tomás and Harvey. Or you're out on your horse." Her eyes pressed into him, a weight pushing against him. He didn't know what to say, but that didn't matter: it was her monologue. "But I've had the same dream twice. It seems you're drowning, and there's some strange woman—I never saw her before—and she's pulling you out of the water, and you don't have any clothes on"—the eyes narrowed and she paused, wiping salt off the glass with her finger and licking it—"but you're saying my name. Once it was at the reservoir, but the last time you were far away somewhere, on a beach, but it wasn't warm. It's funny, I'm never in the dreams I have of you, unless you mention me. . . ." Her coyness had departed, and she looked serious as she spoke, earnest and again the unsettled girl. "The dream scares me, and I wake up feeling sad and lonely. . . ."

Her hands were on the table before her and he could so easily have reached across to them—so easily—but he didn't. He found it safer to observe, inhibition and a sense of baffled wonder and her deflective allusions to secrets keeping him still, making him wait, as if for one more bit of information or permission or approval of his unvoiced desire, and he knew, too, that this alignment, this convergence like planets all lining up with the sun would pass and he would again drift away from her, and he would wait and watch for the next repetition in this cycle, when perhaps it could be more permanent—

"I'm not going to drown," he said.

"Oh, I know. But—someday we'll all die. I mean, I know everybody knows that, but I guess there's a time when we all realize it for ourselves, isn't there? Here I am, almost eighteen—how profound, huh? I've been thinking so much, lately, about everything, and it all seems to be out there in front of me and I'm not sure how to go to it. But you listen to me, you take me seriously and make me feel like I'll do all right, and you don't tell me what to do. I appreciate it, Daniel. That's all."

"Ruby, what's up?"

She smiled. "I'm going to Europe in August. I wish I could pay for it on my own, but I guess I have to take Dad's money. It's Mom's money, really. But then the deal is I go to work for his friend Phil Bishop, who has that ad agency in LA, and I try it for something like six months. Then, I told Mom, I'd think about college after seeing the 'real' world."

"Wow."

"Yeah."

"Sounds like another toast," Daniel said.

"No, no toast for this one," she said, looking down. "But it'll be all right. I like California, and I feel like I've got to get away from here. It's so confusing."

"How's your mother taking it?"

"She's part of the problem. It's like, we get together and we explode. We're too different, and too much alike, I guess. . . ."

"Your mother is a demanding person. She's—"

"She's a witch, an honest-to-God witch!" Her face was suddenly rigid. "She's made her deal with the devil. And you know what else? I think she and Lester are having an affair or something."

"What? But—"

Ruby cut off his protest with a slashing hand motion. "I've got to get away."

They sat quiet for a few minutes and Daniel crunched away on corn chips to occupy his hands. Gradually her face lost its stony anger, and when she again looked up at him her eyes were faintly apologetic, shifting back and forth on his face.

"I didn't tell you," he said, "but you look absolutely beautiful."

With Ruby he lingered at the restaurant for hours, until the evening became too chilly to sit outside and he could see she was cold, though she didn't say anything and seemed content to stay forever. So he drove her home through the dark night, the stars washing their faint light across the desert and animal eyes occasionally glinting from the new weeds along the highway shoulder. As they passed through one narrow spot, where a bosque crowded the road on both sides, a deer appeared, jumping sideways out of Daniel's lane, leaping a fence into the brush. He swerved by reflex and it was all over so quickly he had to say, "Did you see that?"

"Yes," she answered. "A deer."

When they approached the turn to the village and his house, he considered taking her to his place—she would spirit him away—making love all night, then waking to find her beside him in the morning, but he drove by without even slowing—she was only seventeen—and Ruby didn't stir, though she leaned against him, and he thought perhaps she was asleep. Then at her house he stopped the car in the driveway and they saw all the windows were dark. Ruby sat upright and stretched her torso and he could hear her yawning.

"Should I ask you to come in?" she said.

"I don't know—what would I answer?"

"Ha!" she laughed, making no move to get out, and her scent was all around him now, embedding itself deep in his memory as a permanent longing, that scent blending with the air in the cab into an atmosphere of compressed expectation, a full elastic tension of ripeness, contained energy like the air before lightning strikes, that building toward sudden, catastrophic release—yet she seemed insubstantial beside him, vaporous, searing but vague like the sun marking the retina, a hint of blindness—

"Daniel," she said. "I'll be going away so soon."

"I know. . . ."

"Kiss me good night, then."

He leaned toward her and he felt her teeth beneath her

lips, he felt her restraint but her full attention, too. He slid his hand up to her breast, teasing his thumb across the thin fabric over her nipple. "Come home with me," he murmured in her ear, reckless with the *almost* of her momentary acquiescence to his touch.

Ruby pulled away.

"I feel like I should say something," he said.

"No." She sat upright again. "You shouldn't. Listen—you still see me pure. Like a vestal virgin. Let's keep it that way a little longer." She opened the car door. "Good night. Don't get out, I'll let myself in," and she was gone, but her voice had been tight, choked as by a sob when she spoke, and after he saw her go through the door he drove off, not going home but instead pulling off the road by the river and fishing his sleeping bag out from behind the backseat, laying it out on a little hillock overlooking the water and watching the stars pivot slowly across the sky above him.

He woke early the next morning, his sleeping bag dew-soaked, his shoulders sore from the hard ground, and he felt emptied and abandoned, as if she already had tossed him aside and gone away, flown beyond the ocean—as if she had not sat across the table from him and slipped her eyes over that salty-rimmed glass, or leaned against him so dreamily as the truck hurtled across the dark night, or kissed him with that mute, sad longing, as if it were all a dream. The sun had not yet risen, and the sky was that deepest blue after the blackness has fled as stars melt into daylight, that deepest blue when the world looms larger than all reckoning and the sky parodies even the smallest insight, the slightest inching toward awareness.

He crawled out of his bag and dragged it behind him to the car, tossed it into the trunk, then walked to the edge of the hill and pissed down toward the water, shivering as his bladder emptied. He thought of walking the river, checking the mud for tracks or beaver sign, but instead he stood above the slope, looking across the tops of the valley trees at the hills that rose to the north toward the mesas of the ranch, and he spoke, naming the thing he lacked, the abyss within, a universe of estrangement, that place where no sound echoes, no mirror reflects but is forever shifting, like the sky vanishing into its own impenetrable depths: "Ruby," and the word was gone, soaked up by all that mocking space, the desert spreading away from him in huge, deaf solitude.

13.

RUBY HAS PALED AND SHE SITS ON A ROCK with her head bent in her hands, faint and disoriented, and at first she refuses the water he offers her, then she takes the canteen and drinks from it, and in a moment she can look up again. Lester stands off as if she were dangerous.

Daniel squats in front of her and studies her eyes, which are dilated but not glazed. "Are you all right?"

She nods, then says, "I felt faint for a moment. I feel better." He puts his hand on her knee and squeezes it. "You scared me."

"I'm sorry. Sometimes it all comes down on me at once. It's like drowning, it's so panicky. I knew you were there with me, but I was afraid."

"It's strange . . ." he says.

"You felt it too?"

"What is 'it'?"

"It's . . ." She looks at Lester and falls silent.

"We can talk later, if you want," he says quietly. "There's no hurry," and again she nods. "Let's rest a while."

"No, I want to keep going. I'm all right. Really. I am." She stands and walks toward the horses. Daniel lets her go.

Daniel ties his horse to a tree by Boca and follows Ruby around the ruin, which is little more than low rock piles where walls once stood, spread across an acre meadow, and a stone stairway. Patches of snow occupy the deepest shadows. He wants to ask if this is where she expects to find the corpse, but he doesn't have the nerve.

"The dump was over there," Ruby explains, pointing south toward the tip of the mesa, which projects over the ranch like the prow of a ship, three sides nearly vertical. "It's full of arrowheads and pots." The rooms of the pueblo were small, perhaps six feet on a side, and in one of the better-preserved walls they find the remnants of a roof beam. "It was probably wetter then," she continues, "and there were more tall trees." The meadow is narrow and tends north-south, with scrubby oak trees and ponderosas and big piñons on the margin, the very edge of the mountain forest. "I guess it wasn't this kind of transitional vegetation back then—it was more wooded—but they still had to climb down every day for water, though Mom thought there might have been some kind of cistern system." Lester is poking through the dump, while Ruby meanders through the dry weeds and clumpy grass with her eyes to the ground, scanning, Daniel thinks, in that way her mother taught her, sweeping back and forth for several feet to each side and taking small steps, ranging slightly from left to right like a hound on a scent. Then she stops and crosses her arms on her chest as if she's cold and she looks at Daniel.

"Well?" he asks. "What now?"

She looks around, off toward the trees and the rocky ledge, twisting slightly and looking behind her too: her lips part as if to speak. Distress draws her eyebrows together and her face narrows so that her eyes almost seem to cross, her focus drifting inward for a moment as if scanning those inner visions again, scanning for a window through, a remnant, a hint like one of those broken pots, a shard, some sign that Rae had once passed through here, or had returned—

He goes to her, but she turns away, standing almost on her toes to peer into the trees to the north.

"You think this is where—"

"Yes!"

Daniel looks around too. "But he couldn't have driven up here."

"No, I suppose not." Again he sees one wave of that devastating flood wash over her face, but it passes quickly. "I thought . . . I was sure. . . ."

He waits, but she doesn't finish. He sees Lester squatting near the south rim, contemplating the valley, while the oak leaves so lightly quiver in the breeze as they turn from green to orange and red.

"I'm going to walk that way a little bit," Ruby says, nodding to the trees. "I won't be long."

Daniel wants to keep her near, but instead he watches her turn and walk away, moving quickly and jumping one of the slumping walls. She veers to the northeast, where the cliffs of the mesa make a gradual curve on the eastern side until they are running east-west instead of north-south, and soon she is lost in the trees, heading eastward, sunward.

Daniel joins Lester at the dump, where he has assembled a collection of pot sherds at his feet. "I've got about two-thirds of a pot here," Lester says. "But now I can't find the rest." Daniel picks up a few of the pieces, fits them together. "All the king's horses," Lester says. "I'm really going to miss Rae, you know? It's starting to sink in. She really meant a lot to me. She saved me from myself, I think sometimes. She pulled me out of the fire. She bailed me out." He toys with a few of the shards.

"These last few months, she kept her distance, though. When she moved to the Turkey Springs place, she shut everybody out. I don't think she and Calvin saw each other even once a week. I'd go up there to help her with something, and she was real quiet, working through her collection, classifying pieces and writing everything up—she was working on an article for one of the anthro journals, you know."

"No, I didn't."

"Yeah, she seemed excited about that. That was a big step. She had made up her mind about Calvin. I think she didn't know how to do it. The ranch was hers, but she was no rancher. She didn't care for it. I loved her, Dan. We really had some great times together. But we weren't going to get together. It wasn't like that. I guess we'd become more like really good friends than anything else. Really close friends."

They sit a moment, listening to several ravens that have gathered in the trees, then Daniel asks: "Where are the journals?"

"I don't know."

"Ruby thinks you do."

"Ruby thinks a lot of strange things." Lester stands up and turns back to the pueblo ruin. "Where is she?"

"She went for a walk that way."

"I think I might ride back down," Lester says. "I've actually got work to do."

"Go the long way," Daniel says, thinking of descending that steep hill on horseback.

"I will."

"You don't have to go—" Daniel offers, perhaps a bit too late, thinking: Ruby.

"I know it," but they have already reached his horse, and Lester swings into the saddle. "I'll see you—"

Alone then, Daniel walks across the meadow to the east

rim of the mesa, where he can see the snowcapped peaks from Taos down to Santa Fe. He sits on the smooth sandstone, warmed by the sun, so he takes his shirt off and lets it soak in. He closes his eyes and dozes, his eyelids orangey from sunshine and the buzz of the few surviving insects filling his ears and the chattering of irritated ravens—

—*she* says, "Daniel," clearly and loud and close by—

—and he snaps awake and sits up, the ravens still chattering and the insects clicking away, but no one is there: he is alone. He stands. "Ruby?" No one answers. He suppresses the urge to shout her name, thinking how it would echo among the cliffs forever, the countless echoes like hysteria clanging through the brain, corrupting the wordless perfection of wilderness he has thrust himself into, the wilderness where she now sits, somewhere, waiting, like a coyote waiting thoughtlessly for the moon to rise, waiting for that strange irresistible summons, waiting to reply in wordless voice.

Suddenly nervous, restless, overcome by that sensation he has only felt in the desert, that he is closely observed despite the infinite surrounding loneliness, he strikes out north a few steps back from the rim, heading into the thin trees where he saw her last.

She finds him first. As he scuffs through the sand and loose rock, she appears from the rim on his right, calling: "Hi, there!" and he is startled.

"Where have you been?" he asks as they approach each other.

"Oh—" She waves vaguely with her hand to the east.

He studies her face and sees she is relaxed, less distracted than before. Something is settled. "Did you have a nice walk?"

"Yes—it's so beautiful here. I missed this place so much. —I didn't find anything, though."

"I thought I heard you call my name. I guess I dozed off in the sun."

She smiles, an open-mouthed smile, and her tongue plays about her teeth. "Oh? You must have been dreaming."

"Must have."

She has taken off her flannel shirt and tied it about her waist.

"I guess I'm still getting used to being around you," he says.

"Where's Lester?" Ruby asks.

"He went back. He said he had work. . . ."

"I used to ride up here, when I felt like I really needed time alone to think," she says. "It's funny, even with all that's going on, I'm happy right now. Just this second, I'm happy. I feel—I don't know. Alive. You're here. We're here. Mom always said this ranch was a power center. I grew up believing that, and when I left, I began to learn what it really means." Her eyes quiver and shine; she radiates that secret glow of knowledge: "I have a plan."

"What?"

She touches him, then turns and he can't resist following her to a rock, where they sit above the cliffs in the sun. "I'm going to inherit this place, me and Harvey, and Tomás gets part too."

"I heard."

She nods and she is studying him as if his reaction is important. "I'm going to move onto it and rebuild the Turkey Springs place. But you have to come with me. We'll have a family. It will be us, alone. . . ."

—and the spirits, haunting the tree-lined margin, patiently

waiting, watching, in no hurry but ready to seize him, to steal him away into the night forest, running and panting and jostling him, herding him among them, jogging the serpentine path to her garden, fraught with danger, the peril of forgetting, of stepping over and accepting the promise of peace and tranquility in her hollow caves, like wolves, or seals, wolves becoming seals who may dive under without fear—

Thinking a thousand pairs of eyes are watching, he leans to her and kisses her cheekbone, as if in this way the world might be reckoned, his estrangement resolved, the clamoring silenced, her distress evaporated like raindrops on sun-warmed sandstone. "I'll come with you," he says, pretending with her. "Of course—"

There is no one else.

14.

WHEN HE HAD PICKED A DAY to show Rae the petroglyphs, he
invited Ruby to come along, but she declined. He had stopped
by her room, which had its own outside door, one day after
work when high summer was upon them and the cicadas
buzzed in crescendos of orchestrated heat. He had seen her
only once since he took her out the weekend before—she had
become suddenly busy, unavailable, not around—and Rae had
been with her, so he felt shy, though he wanted to ask, to somehow clarify the emotions of that night, to confirm them so at
least his memories might comfort him when she was gone—

He rapped on the screen door, standing in the sun and feeling crusty in his own sweat and his hands greasy from trying
to make the hay baler work. Ruby didn't say anything, but she
came to the door and opened it so he could come inside. She
wore a bathing suit top and running shorts and she looked like
she'd been sunbathing all day.

"God, you're getting tan," he said. She sat on her bed and
continued polishing her toenails while he took a chair at the
little desk that looked out on the fields.

"I wanted to tell you," he said. "I'm moving back to
Albuquerque. I'm going to summer school."

She looked up at him, her eyes soft. "When?"

"Next week. I'll probably go Thursday. I was afraid you might not talk to me before I left."

"Of course I'll talk to you," she said, smiling, but without her customary wattage; rather, she seemed withdrawn, even reticent.

"It seems like maybe you've been avoiding me."

"No. Well—I don't want—I'll be gone, you're going. . . ." She shrugged.

"What are you saying, Ruby, that we can't be friends like we've always been?"

"I'm not saying that. I'm saying . . ."

"How are things with your mom?"

"Oh—the same. Always the same."

"Would you come with us Saturday when we go see those petroglyphs?" he asked.

"No. I can't."

"Why, Ruby?" he asked, annoyance edging his voice.

"Maybe I can't be around you right now. You're . . . too much. I get lost. I get dizzy. Forget it. No: we can't be the friends we've always been. I don't know, Daniel," and her voice abruptly sounded world-weary, a tired bitterness he sometimes heard in Rae's voice. "I'm afraid if I don't go to Europe now and then out to LA . . . Can you understand, and not ask? Because when I get talking . . . I feel like a stupid little girl."

"Ruby," he said, "you're not—"

"No," she cut him off. "Look. I'm eighteen next week. And I have no idea—about anything. I've got to do something on my own. You're a man. It's easy for you. This is something I really need to do."

"Okay," he said, holding up his hands, admitting defeat. "I don't mean to get in your way," and thinking he didn't care if he never saw her again, he left her sitting there on the bed, the nail-polish brush poised over her toes, the cicadas rip-sawing in pandemonium.

The day he was moving out of the little house in the village, heading south to Albuquerque, Rae stopped in to see him as he was packing. He didn't know if she had ever been to the house before, but he wondered if maybe she had visited Lester once or twice in his absence. She came inside and cast a motherly eye around the rooms—checking for cobwebs and dust bunnies, he imagined, or else covering some deeper agitation—and helped him carry boxes out to his car. It was hot and afterward she accepted his offer of a cold drink and they sat in the shade out back, where they could watch the neighbors irrigating their cornfield and see the thunderheads building on the peaks. They had never made it over to the petroglyphs, and Daniel suggested he'd come back some cool fall weekend and they'd go look at them.

Rae perched awkwardly on Lester's old flea-market chaise lounge without really settling into it. "That will be fine," Rae said. "You're welcome back anytime. Tomás is coming back to work for me—for the ranch. But Ruby certainly will miss you," she added, stretching her sandaled foot in front of her and wriggling her toes. Her calf was shapely, slim but well defined. Daniel watched her as she spoke and he saw how much Ruby had come to look like her, though Rae was fair in complexion.

"I'm going to miss Ruby," he said. "Your whole family has been like a second family to me . . ." he added.

"Well, we've been fortunate to have you," she returned quickly, and he thought, Let's get on with this. "Ruby is a confused girl right now," she continued. "She's so easily distracted.

She's like a hummingbird. She has to dip her nose into every flower. I don't think I was ever that fickle. Of course, my mother wouldn't have allowed it. Sometimes I think I've done Ruby a disservice, not being more strict. It's hard, with Calvin." Rae paused a moment, her lips curling in and down at the corners as if tasting something sour. "He believes that anything the kids do is all right, as long as they make it back for breakfast. When I was a child, we called my father 'sir.' But the world is so different. And Ruby is smart—not school smart, like Harvey—she has no patience for that. But I think she understands people—better than I." Her eyes flick to Daniel, then return to the clouds and the mountains. "I misjudge people. I misplace my faith."

"There's nothing wrong with trusting people."

"Yes, sometimes there is. There are some people who can't be trusted—even some you thought you knew very well. But listen: here's what I wanted to say to you. Forgive me. I don't like meddling in other people's lives. You know I'm always the last person to give advice. Wait until she's a woman. You're an adult, Daniel, twenty-one. You have a more adult outlook on life, adult needs, adult responsibilities. Let her be. Let her grow up."

Rae did not look at him as she talked, and he sat back in his chair and watched the clouds swirl and separate and re-form on the mountain. "What makes you think I would do anything else?"

"She's a lovely girl, Daniel. I know how men are."

"Oh, come on, Rae. Give me a little credit."

"I do. Or I wouldn't be here."

"I think you're exaggerating what's between Ruby and me—"

"No."

"She's hardly spoken to me the last few weeks."

"You've obviously upset her."

"I kissed her good night, for chrissakes!" he said, blushing.

"I know. Daniel, ever since she was a little girl, Ruby has always had her own agenda. She makes plans. Calvin is the same way. They are very methodical. They do what they want, and they don't want anyone else telling them what to do. When they decide on something, nobody better get in their way. But Ruby has no idea what her goals are. It scares her. She has a fear of losing out on whatever it is she thinks the world holds for her. I honestly don't know. She has power, and she knows it, but she doesn't know what to do with it, so it doesn't do her any good. It scares me, letting her go off to Europe with a girl-friend. I've tried to help her recognize the danger of her own impulses. That's her little paradox. I think she is fiercely loyal to herself, and that makes her do things that sometimes don't make any sense to the rest of us. Now she's decided on going to Europe and then Los Angeles, and it's her plan, and by God she's going to do it. We had a talk today. She's full of accusation and innuendo. It's all drama for her. She's an angry, mixed-up young woman. I'm telling you all this so you won't be hurt by what she does or doesn't do or say to you. Ruby only wants one thing right now, and that's to go off and be Ruby."

"That's fine with me," Daniel said, still looking off toward the storm on the mountain, the dark clouds now and again pulsing suddenly from a flash of lightning deep inside.

"She doesn't really yet know what to do with men," Rae continued. "You look at her and she seems so mature, so ladylike."

"You're proud of her," Daniel asserted.

"Of course. I want Ruby to go be whatever it is she wants. I still think she's making a mistake not going to college, though. I think she probably never will, but Calvin gave in to her and now it's too late for me to do anything about it. I should have pressed harder on that. They made a deal, and that's it."

"Rae, exactly what is it you want to say to me? What do you want me to do?"

"You have tremendous influence over her. I don't think you realize that. She looks up to you. Don't get in her way. This is such a critical period in her life, when she's telling the whole world who she is, what she is. I don't want her giving up on that future, just yet."

"Neither do I."

"Good," she said.

He wanted to protest, to explain himself, to explain the impossibility he felt with Ruby, but he kept quiet, willing instead to wait for Rae's next words.

"She said she'd be by to see you off around six," Rae said after a minute, and it seemed like her idea, not Ruby's.

"I know. She called."

"Well, I need to be going." She stood from the seat, and Daniel too rose. "Good luck at school," she said, holding out her hand for a formal shake. "Come back to work next summer."

"Yeah. Thanks." He walked her to the door and watched her get into the truck, waving once, then driving down the driveway as Lester turned in. Lester stopped and backed up so she could pull over the cattle guard and they sat there a moment and talked, and Daniel went back to loading boxes into the back of the car and he thought of Ruby sitting there on the bed, polishing her nails.

And when she finally arrived, she was late—it was almost seven, and he had wanted to make the whole drive to Albuquerque in daylight. But when she got out of the car she looked so lovely he didn't care anymore and she came over to him and put her arms around him in a full frontal embrace. They hugged for a good long moment, then stepped apart, and that cold distance he had felt the other day in her bedroom had melted away. They stood and looked at each other for a moment without speaking, then Ruby said, "I promised myself I wouldn't cry," and she smiled—like dawn breaking, a luminous unfolding—so he smiled too.

"No," he said, "no crying. It's not fair."

"How different do you think we'll be the next time we see each other?"

"Not very."

"Really?"

"Really. You'll still be Ruby."

"I'm going to cut my hair. For the trip. Turning over a new leaf."

"You'll look great."

They stood in silence again, then she turned and looked down the driveway and she said, "Will you write to me, if I send you a forwarding address?"

"Yes."

"I'll see you in my dreams," she said, facing him again, a quick smile, then ducking into the car and starting the engine and of course the dreams had barely begun.

Her letters from Europe were lengthy, pages on pages torn from a legal tablet, handwritten descriptions of the Alps, the Adriatic coast, the cathedrals and the small villages she passed through—and he would even sniff the paper sometimes, hoping for some material trace of her spirit—but her words were drawn from a bank of loneliness and emotional isolation, though she would tell him about a disco where she had danced or dinner in a chic Parisian restaurant escorted by a Frenchman with vague ties to royalty, and she often mentioned how Rae would have enjoyed the sites she visited, how her mother would have reveled in the perfect excavation of Pompeii, and she always signed them with *love*, a word Daniel would read and reread as if to memorize the exact shape, then he would store each letter in the front corner of his desk drawer, sometimes pulling out the whole stack to read them again. But he never wrote back, though he drafted many replies in his head.

She called him from London on his birthday, and he had this strange sense it would be her when the phone rang so he surprised her with his lack of surprise when he picked up the receiver and said, "Hello?" and she started singing, "Happy Birthday," and he said, "Ruby, babe, where the hell are you?"

She kept singing, and laughing while she sang, until the first verse was done, then she said, "You sound like you were expecting me to call," her voice fuzzy like cotton over the transatlantic line. "I'm in London."

It was late in the night and he had already gone to bed in his tiny apartment near the university, and it took him a minute to think clearly. "Were you asleep?" she asked.

"No. Just kind of dozing. Hold on a sec . . . So where are you?"

"London. Arlene and I rented a car yesterday and drove to Stonehenge, then down through the countryside. It's a trip driving on the wrong side of the road, but we survived, I guess."

"How'd you like Stonehenge?"

"Great. But I wanted to tell you: we were driving through a little town in Surrey, I think it was, and we're going along this narrow road—you know how they are?—and along these hedges, then we go up this hill and there's an old stone church, from 1540 or something like that, and I had to go in. It was late in the afternoon, and misty and the sun was this incredible orange. . . . So we went inside, and I was standing up near the pulpit and through a doorway I heard this rustling sound, kind of heavy, like something dragging, and I couldn't think . . . I had no idea what it was. It was one of those sounds that grabs you. I can't describe it. Then the bells started to ring. You know, that 'ding-dong, ding-ding-dong, ding,'" she sang the melody, "and I just—ohh! Someone was standing there ringing those bells by rope and I felt like I'd been there before. It was overwhelming." Her voice lowered almost to a whisper. "I cried, Daniel. I stood there and cried. It was dark and Arlene was outside, and I sat down on one of those old wooden pews and it was like feeling your whole family has died, or—I don't know. But I wasn't sad, I was—it was more like empathy. I felt someone else's. . . . It was like having thoughts that aren't yours."

"Are you all right now?"

"Oh, yeah! I'm fine. It was just—a psychotic episode or something. It was so moving. . . . I had to tell you. I couldn't think of anyone else to tell about it. I thought you wouldn't laugh. There's something else I need to tell you. It's important. It's something you need to know about me. But I can't do it on the phone. I thought I could. I'm sorry."

He sat for a moment, not knowing what to say, his feelings blacked out in that familiar here-we-go-again limbo of waiting her out. Then she added, "That little church made me so homesick, too, because for that ten minutes, or whatever, I felt so incredibly connected to that little church in England. The place put its arms around me, the way the ranch does. And I felt like I would be happy crawling under a leaf, crawling under a leaf in the creek, and staring up at the sky, and lying there so quietly."

"Ruby—" he began, thinking it was time to clarify her intentions as she became an adult.

"So, anyhow," she cut in, "how was your day?" Her voice was airy and girlish again, making light of the weight on the phone line, and he wanted to tell her that he loved her, but the word, encoded and stretched by wires and waves of electricity over the ocean, might somehow become scrambled and twisted and deformed: better to wait, to touch, to huddle close in that imaginary streambed, to dare the loneliness for another lifetime of waiting—

"Did I tell you about the guy I met on the Côte d'Azur? He was a descendant of Louis the Fourteenth, or one of those French kings. We were on this topless beach—believe me, I kept *my* top on—and this man about forty with, like, three gold neck chains, comes over to me and Arlene and he sits down on the sand next to us and we're making small talk, and there's this huge yacht—I mean, a real ocean liner—out in the water, and he says, 'Do you like my boat?' And I'm kind of looking around for something like a speedboat, and he says, 'There,' and he's pointing right at it, and I figure this is the richest guy I ever met, and he asked me if I wanted to go sailing with him! He said he had an island off Greece."

"Tempted?"

"No. Yes. No. God, Daniel, he just wanted to fuck me. Excuse my language."

"Yeah, watch it," he kidded.

"I mean, I felt like I needed a pregnancy test after he was done looking me over. It was like Arlene wasn't even there."

"Do you know how beautiful you are, really?"

"Oh, Daniel."

"Let me tell you something about men—"

"I know. I did turn him down."

"Okay."

"Okay."

"I worry about you over there, Ruby."

"You and Mom."

"England should be pretty safe."

"Yeah," she said, and she sounded almost disappointed. "How can I come home after all this? How do you keep a girl on the ranch after she's seen gay Paris?"

"California. That's next, right?"

"Yep."

"When are you coming back?"

"Two weeks."

"I'll see you?"

"Oh, yes, I promise. Bye—"

"Bye."

It took him hours to fall asleep and he lay in bed so long dozing, thinking she was in the room with him, sitting on the bed beside him in the dark describing a seemingly endless adventure in the ocean, and her loneliness.

15.

ON A BRILLIANT BLUE AUTUMN DAY when all the cottonwoods along the river and the streams and arroyos were flashing gold and the lightest of snows dusted the high peaks on every horizon, Daniel drove up from the city to help Lester cut firewood. They borrowed Calvin's old dump truck to creep back into the hills above the decrepit Willard homestead and Daniel began mentally composing a letter that would find Ruby at the hotel in Venice or Geneva, declaring himself, making outrageous offers to satisfy her every desire—and his own. He would tell her how he hated the city, hated going to college, and hated being apart from her.

Instead, when Lester stopped the truck on a high escarpment where the piñon and juniper trees clumped almost like a forest, and they sat on the truck bed to look out across the river and the mesa above it and the deep green valleys toward Turkey Springs, when they had been still long enough to sense the overwhelming depth of time in the land around them, Lester had broken their silence; he had interrupted the wind washing like heavy surf over the compact junipers and piñons and the subtle, imagined *pinging* of sunlight on rock—Lester, the disciple of integrity, had told him not about his own peccadillo but about Ruby's, because it illuminated her state of mind and Lester felt an almost fraternal obligation to expose secrets—and the letter in Daniel's head wisped away from him like leaves on the wind—

And he had said to Daniel, "Ruby came over to my house a few weeks ago," neither ashamed nor embarrassed, "and we smoked a couple joints, some of that really strong dope that Harvey's been growing down in the arroyo," Daniel already grasping the direction of Lester's story.

"Oh, yeah?" Daniel had said as if it didn't matter as if Ruby was simply one of fifty million young women in the Western world. "So'd you get any?" Daniel pressed, and Lester had returned, "No. We kinda cuddled together. Don't you get it, asshole? It wasn't any big deal. She wanted company. So she came on to me. So what? It didn't seem right. It's not like I didn't want to, though. That girl can put a spell on you. But I wouldn't do that. It was too weird, what with me and Rae and all. We talked about you and her mom all night."

"All night, huh?"

"Figure it out, Daniel. She's in love with you."

"No, she isn't."

"Yes, she is." Lester pressed on. "But that's probably why she hasn't slept with you. Sex is a shortcut for Ruby. I've seen it before. It gives her a guy's complete attention. But with you, she doesn't want to cheapen your interest." Lester shrugged. "She needed a friend. It's no big deal," but it was a big deal to Daniel, who wished it had been him she'd sought in the night. But she had been chaste and demur since the night they'd gone out to the restaurant and it seemed clear to Daniel that he wasn't in the running.

Then Lester had jumped off the truck and dragged the chain saw off the bed and they had worked for hours, cutting down dead piñon trees and limbing the trunks and stacking the logs in the truck, hardly speaking except when it concerned the job at hand. Daniel labored hard to outdo Lester and to drown out his private inner clamor.

And later, after they had unloaded the truck at Lester's home in the village above the river, when they sat on the concrete wall of the back porch sweating in the thin, fall air and drinking cold beers, Lester still wanted to talk about it, to make Daniel feel better, assuming his big-brother role.

"She was packing her things to go to Europe, and I'd see her walking back and forth between the barn and the house, and it seemed like Rae wasn't even talking to her, and Harvey was back in school—like you—and she seemed real alone, and we'd talk down by the corral, or she'd ride on the tractor with me to feed horses—you know, we had that little wagon to carry hay in, before Harvey backed it into the tree next to the barn. And she didn't really tell me much about what was going on in her head, only that she'd had a fight with her mom that day, or how excited she was to be getting away, going abroad, but something was going on, something was really eating at her. It was something about Calvin. Something he did a long time ago. I've got my guesses, but . . ."

Lester's face seemed so sad as he talked about Ruby that soon Daniel was waving him quiet, saying, "Man, you don't have to explain anything to me. It's cool, it really is. It's just that, you know, goddamn it, sometime a few years ago Ruby permanently broke my heart, and it always seemed like she was too young, or we couldn't connect, so I try not to think about her that way, and then for you—"

"The thing I'm trying to tell you, Dan, if you'll let me, is don't fuckin' put her off forever."

"What does it matter to you?"

"I love both of you," Lester answered with an utter truth that made Daniel's eyes well with tears while Lester peered out over the top of his beer can, gulping the last swig, but still Daniel had to say, "It hurts, that's all," for all the time gone by. "I feel like I can't be *me* without her."

"You ought to get over that," Lester said.

"Why?" Daniel asked him.

Lester shrugged with his eyes before shifting directions again. "You know the last thing she said to me before she left for Europe?"

"How the fuck would I know?"

"'Don't tell Daniel I came over here.' So here I am, telling you—"

"That's because it's your last chance to be a decent human being," Daniel returned, taking the chance to joke a bit himself, and he slapped Lester on the shoulder as he stepped toward the door, wondering why on earth he had ever quit working for the ranch and Lester stayed.

They went back inside. While Daniel peed away his first and second beers, Lester put a record on the stereo. When Daniel joined him in the living room, Lester joked, "Who was Elizabeth Reed, anyhow?" referring to the title of the Allman Brothers jam shaking the hardwood floors of the house. "She must have been sweet, that's for sure, for ol' Dicky Betts to cook like this." They stood and listened to the guitar solo, a great, raw electric wailing, then Duane Allman took over, the notes at first subtle, then keening, running back over themselves, stabbing, building toward a relentless crescendo, then falling back into a long muffled staccato introverted phrase and finally hammering onto a repeated note, trilling on sixteenth notes pounding the point home, but Daniel could not let the issue die as he thought of Ruby dragging a train of admirers across the plazas of Italy. "Like mother, like daughter, I suppose . . ." he said to Lester, whose musing smile vanished and his face turned hard, suddenly older and even dangerous. "Let that lie, man. Don't even talk about it."

16.

EVERY FOURTH OF JULY, Calvin and Rae held a barbecue, inviting all the neighbors and everyone who had ever run cattle in the area or helped Rae on the dig and all the friends of the kids, too. On a glorious blue day after Daniel's year back in college, after Ruby had returned from Europe and gone to California without visiting him, he drove the two hours north, back to the place that had crept under his skin and mixed with the blood of his veins.

Right away he spotted Ruby, standing idly in the shade of a tree smoking a cigarette and watching him drive up while Harvey poked the cook fire around with a broken branding iron, so Daniel drove to the tree—he was early, and others wouldn't arrive for a couple hours—and she walked toward him as he parked.

"How long are you here for this time?" he asked as he got out, but she ignored him for the moment and they embraced and he slid his hand around on her back for the sensation of feeling her, to know that it really was Ruby.

"Just the weekend." Her eyes, as dark and dense as he imagined the universe must have been before the command for light, a burdened dark emptiness of potential, of compressed time—

her eyes stared into his for a moment, then slipped away, toward the house and the cookout, where Daniel saw another man now helping Harvey place the grill over the fire, each wearing a heavy long-cuffed glove and gripping the metal with pliers.

"You're not alone?" he asked.

"No." She sighed. "You can meet David in a minute. He's nice. I think you'll like him."

"Sure."

"Can you stay the weekend?" she asked then, her hand brushing his arm, then settling back to her side.

"I was hoping to."

"Stay in the bunkhouse."

"All right."

They stood and looked at each other and Ruby was smiling, all white teeth.

"You look great," he said. "Been on the beach?"

"A little. It's so good to see you."

"You're smoking. . . ."

"Yeah. I'm going to quit. How come you never come to visit?"

"How come you never asked me to?"

"I figured you wanted to be alone, you know, doing whatever it is you do alone," she retorted, a brief teasing wickedness narrowing her eyes to slits. "Away from everybody."

"You think I'm antisocial?" he came back, but he was kidding too. "I moved to the city, now, didn't I?"

"You did," she said, and she wasn't smiling anymore. "You sure as hell did."

He leaned back against his car and closed his eyes, soaking a bit of sun, and he said, "It's summer again, at last."

"It's always summer in California, it seems," Ruby said,

and when he opened his eyes she was stubbing the cigarette out with her toe.

"How are things going out there?" he asked.

"Pretty well. I'm working part time now. I don't know. I've been going to a counselor. You know, talk about my troubled childhood." She rolled her eyes as if exasperated by the melodrama. "It helps, though. Someday I've got to confront them, my parents, my dad. . . . So I think about coming back here sometimes, but I don't know what I would do. Waitress, maybe—that's such a drag. Guys always hitting on me."

"What does David do?" he asked, nodding toward the man working around the fire with Harvey.

"Oh. He's a guitar player. He does studio work—you know, jingles and things like that. Plays on people's records. He's a genius, I guess."

"You sound so enthusiastic," he said, but she shook her head as if she didn't want to talk about it.

"He brought a guitar. Maybe he'll play later," she said.

"Should we go down and see if we can help?"

"Okay," and she put her arm around him for a quick squeeze and they cut across the grass toward the house, the cookout, and this man who—mesmerized, Daniel thought, like all the others—had followed Ruby to El Rancho de las Animas: all lost souls here, he and Lester had always joked.

"Is Les here yet?" he asked.

"Oh, yeah. He and Dad ran out to Turkey Springs for the picnic tables."

"I'd like to go out there while I'm up here," Daniel said.

"Maybe we could all camp out on the river."

"Let's do it," he urged as they reached the cook fire.

Harvey came over first and shook hands with Daniel.

"Hey, Dan," he said. "We gotta get out for a ride while you're here. Your horse told me he's pissed off at you."

"I know it."

David stepped forward then, a small, lightly built man, perhaps twenty-four, with a gold-stud earring and neat, short hair, but as Daniel took his hand in greeting he felt the strong grip of a guitarist and noticed his arms were veined and muscular.

"I'm David Guerin."

"Glad to meet you. I'm Daniel Stewart."

"I know. Ruby talks about you all the time."

"It's probably all lies," Daniel joked.

"I don't think so," David said straight-faced, and Ruby was conspicuously silent, standing off to the side, watching, and Daniel waited for the moment to pass, feeling he had no place to put his hands, until Harvey said, "Come on, Daniel. Let's go get some more wood. There's a stack of oak by the barn," and as they separated into pairs Ruby's eyes locked onto his own, crowded with an inarticulate mix of affection and sadness, and he felt a magnetic pull to be near her, but instead he got into Calvin's truck with Harvey and they drove down the road to the barn, dust swirling cloudy behind them, and in the mirror he could see Ruby and David step through the screen door into her room.

"Seems like a nice guy," Daniel said.

"Yeah."

Then later, after they had stacked wood and made sure the fire was going well, Rae held out her arms as he came in the kitchen and she pecked him on the cheek. "Welcome back, stranger," she said, and he felt slightly embarrassed by her unusual display of affection. Rae had a huge pot of beans on the stove and she was slicing up fresh loaves of bread.

"You're really setting out a spread," he said.

"It's only once a year, as Calvin is constantly reminding me. Everyone has a good time. Noblesse oblige, I suppose— show everybody we're not snobs. Sit down. Talk to me while I cook." Harvey had disappeared. "I went looking for your petroglyphs, but I couldn't find them. Are you sure you didn't imagine them?"

"Yep."

"Well. And I've found a second stratum at Turkey Springs, a pit house under the pueblo. I think there's a chamber underneath. I've been waiting for Lester to finish haying the river pasture so he can help me move this one great big stone"—she gestures to indicate its size, spreading her hands as wide as her arms will allow—"so I can get down into it." She speaks rapidly, with animated hands, molding the air into the shape of a sandstone slab, an underground cavern. "But there are so many things happening now, I can't get to it. Have you seen Ruby?"

"She was a one-woman welcoming committee."

"I wish she was a one-man woman."

"She's doing all right."

"No. I think she's using drugs, Daniel," and he thought, I wish I had a dollar for every time I saw Ruby smoke a joint. "It makes me very, very angry. I hope you'll be able to talk to her while she's here."

"I can't tell Ruby anything. . . ."

"You tell her what's in your heart, and you might be surprised."

But Daniel sat quiet and thought of David's strong fingers and veined arms and delicate, precise fingertips on Ruby's dark, glossy skin.

Then they saw Calvin and Lester drive by the window with picnic tables stacked on the dump truck and Daniel said,

"I better go help them unload," and she said, "I'll send Harvey too."

As he helped Lester set one table to the ground, Lester asked if Rae had told him about the underground chamber.

"Yeah, actually. She sounded pretty excited." Calvin had gone inside to answer the phone and Lester sat down on the table and wiped sweat off his face with a handkerchief. He never wore a hat and his face was burned a deep red.

"She's afraid to open it," he said, holding his work gloves in his hand and slapping them against his thigh with a rhythmic twist of his wrist.

"She said she was waiting for your help."

"Well, she's afraid to open it. Some kind of Neolithic voodoo. I've seen her out there at night. She'll sit against one of the walls by the vault, by that slab of rock over the top, and sometimes I think I hear her talking. Goddamn, Daniel, it gives me the creeps. I get so I halfway believe her. It makes me think of some old movie, you know, *The Curse of the Ancient Pharaohs*, or something like that, with Peter Lorre." Daniel laughed, but Lester said, "I'm serious, man. You know Tomás won't even work out there anymore."

"You're out there a lot?"

"I'm out there a lot." His steady blue eyes held Daniel's for a moment, then he said, "She's living out there now. All the time."

"She always went out there in the summer."

"Well, this time it's different. She digs, and she writes, and most of the time she won't even talk."

"What about Calvin?"

"You know Cal, man. He's so fuckin' busy runnin' around the ranch he doesn't know she's gone. No. That's not true. I don't know, Dan my man. I don't know. I do my thing and try not to hurt anybody. Sometimes I work with Father Raymond in his garden—to get quiet, to get away from all this bullshit—but then I get thinking about Rae across the river there, and I have to go back and be around to help her. What can I tell you? It's a lot of craziness right now."

"Always is."

"Always is. Speaking of which, Ruby—"

"Don't even tell me."

"Right."

They sat a while in the bright midday. The air was sharp and clear. Every rocky detail of the cliffs to the north stood in vivid relief. "It's gonna be a hot one," Daniel said.

"Why don't you move back up here?"

"I don't know, Les. It's like sleeping on a bed of nails, you know? Seeing her here, with this other guy around. I don't need this torture."

"Why don't you do something about it?" Lester asked. "Why don't you load her into your car and head south?"

"Why don't we unload this other table and go check my horse."

"Right."

17.

TOMÁS ARRIVED EARLY for the Fourth of July picnic. Daniel was in the kitchen helping Harvey load platters with steaks and burgers and kebobs and corn on the cob wrapped in foil to stick down in the coals for ferrying to the barbecue pit. Tomás came in without knocking and hugged Ruby and said, "How are you, *mijita*?" They talked quietly a moment in the living room. When Calvin came in through the front door, Tomás stood back and the two men nodded at each other without expression, then Rae appeared from the bedroom hallway and the atmosphere felt as charged as imminent lightning. Harvey grabbed a plate of meat and headed for the door, Daniel right behind. With their free hands they lugged between them the giant metal thermoses of iced tea and lemonade. After they got these things laid out on tables, they set up the beer keg in the back of Calvin's truck, tapped it, then drank down a few quick cups with Lester in the shade until the neighbors started to drive up in station wagons and pickups crowded with kids and wizened old ranchers with pencil mustaches and neatly creased straw cowboy hats, so that soon they were so busy cooking—flipping steaks and burgers and fishing out the corn with long tongs—that they barely had time to gulp down something cold between waves of hungry partygoers.

When he could, Daniel watched Ruby, standing with David a step or so behind her, as she talked to some old high school flame or one of her friends from town, girls who never left home and now worked at Safeway or the video store next to Lotaburger, one even with a baby at her hip, and they drank beer from the red plastic cups and they told Ruby how their boyfriend had gone off to join the marines or moved to Albuquerque to work construction—or so he imagined they said, letting out small bits of their lives under the impeccable blue sky—and Ruby would listen with apparent concentration drawn from some deep reserve of empathy before moving on to someone else, working the party like a trained hostess but with sincerity, too. Then around one thirty, after the first round was over and all the kids were coming back for seconds, she came through the line with two plates while Daniel poked at the steaks and said, "How do you like 'em?" and she tartly replied, "You know how I like 'em: so rare they're horny," and he had to laugh.

"Where's David?"

"He went to get his guitar. He got talking with Lester and decided he'd jam with his picker buddies. Bluegrass is really his thing, you know, and he hardly ever gets to play it."

"Good. I'd like to hear him."

"Why don't you come eat with us?" she asked. "We've got a spot out behind the house, where the hammock is."

Behind him Daniel heard Lester say, "Go ahead. Me 'n' Harv can handle it from here. Looks like everybody's got something. We're gonna eat pretty soon too."

"All right," Daniel said, grabbing food for himself. "I'll follow you," and with his eyes riding on the back pockets of her jeans he walked across the grass and down the driveway alongside the house to the backyard above the arroyo, where a big globe willow threw afternoon shade outside the window of Ruby's room. Daniel picked a shaky lawn chair and Ruby sat cross-legged beneath the tree, and he could hear Calvin and Rae talking in the kitchen, their voices pitched too low to hear except Rae saying, "Tomás," and while he had Ruby alone, before anyone else intruded, he said, "How are things going, Rube, really?"

"Don't listen to my mom," Ruby answered, cutting into the meat on her plate. "She has wild imaginings of my life-style—out in Hollywood, the land of temptation and vice and the permanent corruption of innocent young maidens. So I lay out in the sun and read trashy paperbacks. What else is new? I'm safer out there. David's the straightest guy I know. He won't let cocaine into the house."

"Are you living with him?"

"No." Her eyes were coyly ambivalent, and he wondered which evasion they urged him to uncover.

"You know, sometimes I want to move back here so badly it's like a physical ache. But they want to promote me at work, and I'm starting to get my own accounts and make pretty good money, and I have friends there. When I get around my old friends from here, I have nothing in common with them. Maybe I never did. Except you. I miss you, Daniel."

"You're one of my favorite people in the world, Ruby," he managed to say, and they fell silent as the wind stirred the willow, and then they could hear the melodic tapping sound of David playing warm-up scales on an acoustic guitar in Ruby's room and Daniel wondered if he had overheard their conversation. He said nothing more, and in a few minutes David joined them, a handsome old Martin guitar in his hand. He gently leaned the instrument against the wall in the shade, then sat against the tree and took up the plate Ruby had for him.

"They'll bust me out of the union if they hear about this gig back in LA," he said, and Daniel laughed. David crunched into his corn, then added: "This dry climate is tough on guitars. I was playing in the sun a little while ago and I had to tune it every few minutes."

"It's tough on everything," Daniel suggested. "Too dry, too hot in the summer, too cold in the winter." David watched him as he spoke, holding his eye, only looking to his food when Daniel paused. "But you've always got to take into account the sun."

After chewing a mouthful, David said, "Ruby has a picture of the ranch, a beautiful sunset on the cliffs—she said you gave it to her—framed on her living room wall. Everybody who comes to the house goes over and looks at it. I've noticed that. Have you?" he asked Ruby. "Everyone goes over and kind of studies it, like, 'Wow, that's unreal!' It almost doesn't look like this planet. Now that I see it in the flesh, so to speak, I don't see how you could ever go away if you came from here."

Ruby was silent, stirring the steak around on her plate without taking a bite and then, once, shooting a glance up at Daniel—

—an apology, or a quick-passing revelation of some secret desire, as if only he could fulfill—

But then she popped a bite into her mouth and, while chewing, shook her hair back from her shoulders and tilted her face into the sun, which slipped through a gap in the tree branches, and she said, "You can feel it burning, here. It feels like a fire—"

—or a foretelling, a glance ahead through the stream of time—

Daniel sat a while in silence while David cleaned his plate and Ruby stretched out on the grass, then Lester and Harvey joined them, and Lester said, "Hey, did you decide to play with us?" gesturing to the guitar, and David nodded with his mouth full.

"All right!" Lester said.

"When are you guys going to start?" David asked.

"Oh, we usually set up around five or so, when it starts to cool off. Everybody's gonna wander off and find a tree to nap under right now. There's a fiddler coming from Ojo, and a pretty hot steel player from Santa Fe, a friend of mine from the old days."

Lester had finished eating, and he stood and walked over to David's guitar. "That's an old Martin D-18."

"Sure is," David said.

Lester reached toward it, then dropped his hand.

"Go ahead," David said.

Lester hesitated. "It looks like Clarence White's," referring to the legendary bluegrass virtuoso who also had played with the folk-rock band the Byrds.

"It is Clarence White's," David answered.

Lester stared at him a moment. "You're kidding!"

"No. I bought it from his estate."

"Man! The Kentucky Colonels, the Byrds . . ." Lester trailed off in visible amazement.

"Yeah, he was great. He mentored me a little, I guess you could say."

"Sure you don't mind?" Lester pressed.

"No, really."

"God, I always wanted one of these," Lester said with true admiration. He picked up the old guitar, then squatted and rested it on his thigh, running his hand up and down the neck. Then he tried a few notes. "The action on these . . ."

"Yeah. It's the sweetest thing."

Lester looked around at Daniel and Harvey. Ruby seemed asleep on the grass. He set the guitar down again, as if it were too valuable for his dirty hands, resting it lightly on its cloth against the wall and checking that it wouldn't slide over. "Nice."

"Thanks. Ruby tells me you've got all kind of horses on this ranch," David said suggestively.

Harvey picked up on his hint. "You want to go for a ride?"

"Sure. I'd love to."

Harvey looked over at Daniel as if to say, "We'll give this dude a ride," but all he said was, "We can go out in a while. Hey, Ruby?"

Her eyes opened a crack and she said, "No, thanks. Maybe tonight. Why don't you men go."

"All right," Harvey said; then, to David: "Let's make it about an hour." And Daniel nodded to indicate he too would go along, but his eyes were on Ruby's supine figure on the ground, the flaring of her hips, the taut brown skin where her belly button showed between her shirt and pants, her hair splayed out on the ground—

Daniel left the others lounging around on the lawn and went into the house to use the bathroom, and when he cut through the living room, Rae was lying on the couch with a damp washcloth on her forehead and the curtains drawn tight. Sometimes she would be immobilized by headaches. He remembered when she had gotten those curtains, backed by a heavy vinyl so it would be dark as night when she wanted to rest. He paused when he saw her, but her eyes flickered and he knew he was detected.

"Sorry, Rae."

"No, it's all right. I think I took too much sun out there. I'm all right now."

"I was headed for the john."

Her arm dangled listlessly over the side of the couch and her hand hunted, then settled on a glass with half-melted ice sitting on the floor. She lifted it and said, "Would you—"

"Fill it? Sure." He stepped toward her and took the glass and her eyes looked glazed. From the kitchen, he called, "More ice?"

"Please." When he returned, she was sitting upright. "Thank you." She sipped. "Sit down," and, forgetting his earlier mission, he obeyed.

"Is everyone enjoying himself?" she asked.

"I think so. It's a great event. Sort of tribal . . ."

"Exactly," she agreed, and her eyes kept him seated. "It's good to have you around again, Daniel." He nodded. "Why don't you move back? Help Lester out with the fieldwork."

"It would be nice," he admitted, as if discussing an impossible fantasy. "But I've got to finish school, get my degree."

"You're so grown up." Rae sighed. She sat forward. "I had an archaeologist from Denmark out here," she said, abruptly shifting the conversation. "He had done work in Iceland. Historical archaeology—so different from what I do. They still believe in elves and trolls and such things there. He had also done a Norse excavation in Greenland, but his major work was outside Reykjavik. He said they have a story for every rock, every hill and river in the landscape. We've lost that, haven't we? The legends . . . It's our loss. But there's no going back. Yet we're deformed by it, I think. Now, instead of bending with the world, it bends us. At Turkey Springs . . . Well, I'd better get back to my party. Calvin's idea of being a host is sneaking a cigar with a couple cattlemen behind the barn."

They stood together, and she said, "This house is yours. Make yourself at home."

When he returned outside, the others had left, the guitar gone too, and instead of hunting for them he settled into the hammock, which hung from a metal frame in the shade of a huge tamarisk that grew on the edge of the arroyo. After a heavy summer rain, the arroyo would run full, and often he had enjoyed lying in the hammock, listening to the brown water chuckle against the rocks, but this day it was sandy dry, and silent, and he fell asleep to the distant sound of horseshoes clinking somewhere in the orchard.

He awoke when he felt the hammock gently swinging from side to side, and he opened his eyes to see Ruby standing over him, nudging it with her knee. Behind her was only the cobalt blue, and he was still slightly groggy, so he said, "I kissed you once, didn't I?"

"Yes. Once. On the lips, that is."

"We're two strange people, Ruby."

"Too strange . . ."

"What if I did come to California?"

She pursed her lips as she considered his question, then said: "Not yet," her voice breathy.

"No," he agreed. "I couldn't live there, anyhow."

"No."

"Maybe we could meet somewhere, like . . . the Grand Canyon."

"Then what?" Her head turned so she could regard him slightly askance. But in the corner of his eye he saw David round the corner of the house, his head down in a concentrated stride. "Here's your friend," Daniel said, retreating from her query, or more precisely from his answer, which might finally clarify his position, and hers too. Ruby turned to watch David approach, as she might watch a child. "Isn't he cute?"

David apparently heard this last question and said, "Who?"

but Ruby didn't answer, returning instead her gaze downward to Daniel and saying, "Yes. Let's—"

"Lester and Harvey are bringing in the horses," David said, oblivious to their momentary intimacy.

"Okay," Daniel said, and he swung his legs to the ground. "You comin,' Ruby?"

"No. I'm going to see Mom." She turned and headed for the back door, and David said, "I better go put some jeans on," and Daniel called after her, "Ruby?" She stopped and turned. "Actually, it was twice."

"Twice?" she asked.

"New Year's."

She laughed lightly. "Oh, I know!" Then she spun and vanished through the door.

18.

ON WINTER BREAK FROM COLLEGE six months ago, Daniel had driven up the day after Christmas and stayed in the house with Lester, and they had Harvey and Ruby over for dinner, eating the remnants of a turkey Lester had cooked for his girl-friend from Taos who stood him up Christmas Eve because she was a Buddhist, she said, and they sat around the stove and talked about old times and Ruby told stories about her Europe trip or the skateboarders in LA, and Harvey drank too much and got very quiet, and Daniel wondered if Lester was sleeping with Rae, whose presence lurked around the room, though she never accompanied her children when they came over to the house.

Then he went with Les up to the ranch for New Year's Eve, a traditional night when Calvin and Rae had a few friends in to eat posole and drink punch and champagne and try to stay awake till midnight.

Lester was stone quiet for the drive. They left shortly after dark, a night so cold their breath seemed to crystallize as they exhaled, but the ground was bare and the stars so brittle Daniel felt if he spoke too loud they might shatter and sprinkle to the ground like snowflakes. At the ranch, Lester mumbled about going down to the barn to look the early foal over, so Daniel approached the front door alone and through the big picture window he saw Ruby in a green holiday dress wrapping her like cellophane. She was standing alone in front of the fire, wine-glass in hand, waiting, it seemed, no one else in the room. He stopped in the cold darkness and watched her wait, motion-less, in the decorated, yellow-lit room, pine boughs hanging from the chandelier above the kitchen table, Christmas cards propped on the mantel over the fireplace, a big spruce tree hung with ornaments and winking white lights, and she was an apparition, a spirit of unearthly beauty, and the sight of her filled him with an ache not of desire but nostalgia for an opportunity sharply considered, then abandoned. He wanted the choice again.

He stepped to the door and rapped lightly so she would know he was coming, and as he went inside she was there to greet him.

"Mistletoe," she said, pointing up.

"Uh-oh."

"Yep," and before he could take his coat off she was kiss-ing him, not quickly but for the enjoyment of it, and his hands settled to her hips. Then she dropped her hands from behind his head and said, "Come on in. Here," she took his coat, "I'll put this in Mom and Dad's room," and she was gone down the hallway and Harvey was coming toward him with two Dos Equis bottles in his hand, saying, "Drink one of these. It'll cure what ails ya."

"I doubt it," Daniel returned. Harvey laughed like he knew exactly what he meant, so Daniel added, "Your sister's gonna be the death of me." Harvey shook his head and Ruby came back in the room and said, "What are you saying about me?"

"Am I the first one here?" Daniel asked.

"No way," Harvey said. "Dad and Tomás are shooting pool, and you couldn't get Criselda out of the kitchen with the front-end loader."

"Where's your mom?"

"She went down to the barn to check the foal."

"Oh. So what do we do now?" Daniel asked.

"Well . . ." Ruby said, and she looked at Harvey, who raised his eyebrows and held his thumb and index fingers, pinched, to his lips as if he were smoking a roach.

"Shall we retire to my room for a few moments?" Ruby suggested with mock formality.

When they came back to the main house, a few more guests had arrived. Rae was showing Lester a framed print Calvin had given her for Christmas, the *Black Cross, New Mexico*, a massive, brooding shape towering above the rippling hills in orange and black. Daniel heard her saying, "It is this place. She's captured it, that inconsolable agony. I often wish I was Catholic. Not being one sets up a barrier with the old Spanish families here."

"Like Tomás and Criselda?" Lester asked.

"Yessss," she hissed.

Lester held the print at arm's length to study it. "It's so dark," he concluded, while Ruby came into the room and took in their dialog, then turned away and headed for the kitchen, Daniel following her, catching up in the hallway, catching her arm even, but she shook him away and called to Criselda, a false brightness gilding her voice, "Can I help in here, *tía*?"

Daniel spent the evening talking horses with the men and telling the ones he knew well how he'd spent the last several months, while Ruby stuck to the margins of the crowd, even disappearing entirely around eleven, but when Calvin whistled his cow-herding whistle and held up his hands to get everyone's attention, Daniel saw her standing partway down the hall. Calvin said, "It's almost midnight," his face ruddy from alcohol and his voice even gentler than usual. "I propose a toast," holding up his glass and other partyers scrambling for a refill so they could partake in the well-wishing.

"To—To, uh—" and everybody laughed at his sudden oratorical lapse, except Rae, whose gaze Daniel followed across the room and into the hallway to settle on an equally unmoved Ruby: the two women regarded each other like intimate enemies. Daniel looked away to find Lester's eyes on him, so he raised an eyebrow, but Lester shook his head, and Daniel realized what he and Rae had been doing down in the tack room earlier this evening.

Then the ball fell in Times Square in a taped replay on television. While everyone hooted, Daniel squeezed sideways through the crowd and caught up with Ruby as she stepped out the back door, still walking as he said, "Don't put me off, Rube. What's going on?" He followed Ruby into her room again. She sat quickly on her bed, hugging her arms across her chest as if she were cold.

"Tell me," he said.

"God, I feel like I'm going to be sick."

"Really?"

"All that champagne and tequila."

"Why don't you lie down."

She obeyed, lying on her side and curling her legs up while he pulled a blanket over her, then sat in the chair. After a few minutes of staring into space, she said, "Don't make me talk about it."

"What?"

"Them."

"Who?"

"My parents: Dad I can handle now. He knows not to cross me, but I think Mom's really losing it, Daniel. So she accuses me . . ."

"She loves you."

"She says, 'Why don't you go to college? Why don't you do something useful?' I'm *working*. She says, 'How many men have you slept with?' She wants a number. She thinks I'm obsessed with sex. And she comes in from the barn, and Lester comes in, and you can practically smell it on them." She kept her eyes away from him and in a few minutes her breathing had calmed. "I'm leaving tomorrow. It's awful. . . . Why won't you come visit?"

"You never asked," he says, and in wounded pride finds cover for his ambivalence, the nagging awareness having grown more insistent these last six months that merely wanting her spared him the risk of discovering who he might be in having her, and the even deeper risk of her discovering him. But maybe she already knew.

19.

DANIEL, LESTER, AND HARVEY TOOK DAVID riding horses across the home pasture, showing him how to neck-rein, how to keep his boot heels down in the stirrups and sit deep in the saddle. On the flats where the footing was good they loped along the deeply grooved and braided cow paths, stopped at the creek so the horses could drink, then walked and trotted back to the corrals. Up at the house they filled their cups from the keg and stood around and talked about other rides they had taken, about riding bucking horses and horses that fell off hills and reared over backward and jumped into barbwire fences. David laughed and shook his head like he couldn't believe there were cowboys who still really did this kind of thing anymore.

Then Lester saw his band buddies drive up in a dusty, oxidized blue Oldsmobile Vista Cruiser station wagon and he took David off to meet them and set up the small sound system and lights on the makeshift stage of plywood sheets laid out on cinder blocks. When they finally started to play, heavy clouds had rolled in from the west and the air went limp anticipating rain, but the players jumped into a traditional Irish tune that Daniel recognized but couldn't name, and people gathered around them on the front lawn of the house, some sitting down, the men hovering at the edges with their arms folded, their heads still bent in conversation. David played rhythm chords and watched the other players for cues and they were all smiling and having a good time jamming. Daniel didn't see Ruby anywhere and he figured she must be in the house, so he and Harvey sat on the side of the truck to listen.

On the second tune, Lester took a solo, flat-picking his way through it and trading bars with the fiddler. Daniel thought how easy it was to see they'd played together for years, each echoing and extending the other's phrasing, sometimes antici- pating the next riff and playing it in unison and laughing at the same time, bobbing their heads and people on the grass clap- ping and whooping to keep them going. When the song ended, Harvey and Daniel clapped loud with their hands over their heads and Harvey leaned to him and said, "Don't you wish you could play like that?"

"I wish I could play, period," Daniel answered. "There's Ruby." He pointed. "Let's go sit with her," so they walked across the grass while the music started again. She looked up smiling as they joined her. Dusk began to blur the edges of the house, the outline of leaves against the sky, the faces across the lawn, but still it didn't rain. They kept playing into the dark, and Ruby leaned against him for a while during a slow, bluesy ballad about a Mexican outlaw. David took the solo, pulling and bending long, fat notes out of the guitar and twisting the melody around like it were a rubber hose. In the dim porch light Daniel could see Lester intently watching the other man play. David stood still and only his hands moved, his face expressionless, tilted up toward the sky. Then the song ended and there was a polite splatter of clapping and Daniel said, "He's incredible," almost hating to admit it but filled with admiration, too.

"He is, isn't he," Ruby said, still resting against Daniel's side.

"Sometimes I think he plays over my head." David plucked out a few notes and twisted the pegs at the top of the neck to tune the guitar again after all that string-bending, and Daniel wondered if he could see Ruby so warm and comfortable at his side, wondered if he would be jealous of the way she set her body so familiarly upon his own in the balmy night air. Harvey had stretched out beside them, his head pillowed on his hands, eyes closed, hat on the grass.

"Whaddya think, Harv?"

"He kicks ass."

"You oughtta be a critic for *Rolling Stone*."

"What I oughtta be is drinkin' a beer," he said, but he made no move to get one.

"Comfortable?" Ruby asked Daniel.

"Yeah. You?"

"Ever so."

"I meant it," he added.

"What?"

"The Grand Canyon."

"Mmmm," she purred.

And he thought, How absurd it all is, the man onstage comping rhythm chords to a hillbilly cover of "Cowgirl in the Sand" and I'm the one sleeping alone tonight. But he stayed with her anyhow, even when she put her head on his shoulder, until the musicians quit playing, setting their instruments down on chairs or in their cases. Daniel stood, stretching, and said, "I'm going to find someplace to sleep," and Ruby looked up and seemed poised to speak, but she only said, "Good night."

"Yeah," he said, adding: "G'night, Harv."

"See you in the morning. Let's ride real early."

"I'll wake you."

And he left before David reached them, because he couldn't stand the thought of watching Ruby lead David to her room.

That night, Lester came and found Daniel in the bunkhouse before he had gone to sleep and said, "Let's go camp at the Rincón," where the flats rose up to a point above a crook in the river. "Harv's up for it."

Daniel only thought a moment before saying he'd do it, and he went outside to get his sleeping bag and ground cloth out of his trunk. They all climbed into the Scout and Harvey said, "Do we have beer?"

"Yeah," Lester said, and Harvey gunned it so the rear wheels kicked out sand and they squirmed down the road past the house, where Daniel saw a light in Ruby's room, the dim green-glass banker's light she kept by her bed.

"Give me one, then," Daniel said, and Lester peeled a can loose from its soft plastic yoke.

"Don't take it so hard," Harvey said to him.

The headlights punched out patches of sandy road from the night. Harvey drove so fast the truck sometimes left the ground on big bumps after they had crossed the highway and were heading over open pasture, not following any track but cutting cross-country along cow paths. Occasionally cotton-tails would dart into the headlights and freeze, sitting stupidly upright as if waiting for the wheel. Harvey would stab the brakes and swerve and sometimes he managed to miss them, but Daniel's mind was stuck remembering the times Ruby had sneaked out with them on midnight rambles like this one, those spur-of-the-moment camping trips to some favorite spot way out on the ranch somewhere, then hurrying home at dawn.

"We shoulda kidnapped Ruby," he said from the backseat. "Made her come out with us."

"She woulda come," Harvey said. "I didn't figure you really wanted us to ask them, though."

"No," Daniel agreed. "You're right." Lester was quiet and stiff in the front passenger seat, holding a beer to his chest and staring into the blackness beside him. Daniel was feeling reckless from the beers and said, "What's with you, Les?" He felt Harvey go tight and Lester didn't answer, so Daniel added, "Harv, you've got some crazy women in your family."

"Don't I know it," he said.

They reached the campsite without wrecking—Harvey was known for his bad driving and he'd totaled Calvin's Ford LTD driving home late from a football game the previous fall—and they threw down their sleeping gear and each wandered off in a different direction for firewood. The trees were sparse here. Daniel walked a hundred yards or so along the ridge above the river thinking about what he should have said before he found a dead piñon with branches he could break off to burn. After he cracked away a few of the limbs he stopped and listened to the quiet under the overcast sky. The night hung close and vaporous like a gauzy web of condensed consciousness: he could only hear the river—it was out of sight—and he couldn't see the cliffs of the ranch five miles away or a single light there, or on the highway, or the hamlet of Polvadera across the river, another five miles—the night hung close as if the hills were waiting, at peace, waiting, even the animals lying close, huddled down in the grass breathing out their unconditional, vaporous breath.

He stood there a while, soaking in the peace, until he heard Harvey calling: "Daniel? Y' all right?"

Daniel said, "Yeah. Comin'," and he had forgotten all about her for two or three minutes.

"Boys' night out?" Ruby asked when he went into the kitchen with Harvey and Lester the next morning.

"What are you doing up so early?" Harvey asked. It was barely seven thirty.

Ruby shrugged. "I do what I please," and her tone silenced any more questions along that line, so Daniel stood on the threshold behind Lester and wondered if he would even stay long enough for coffee, but then her eyes found him and he wished for amnesia.

"Where's Mom?" Harvey asked.

"She's got a headache."

"David?"

"Asleep," she says dismissively.

"Dad?"

"Dunno." She shrugged again and her eyes clicked back on Daniel. She softened her tone to ask, "Do you want coffee?" seeming to ask only Daniel, so he nodded that he did and stepped past Harvey to get a cup from the cabinet next to the sink. She poured for him while the others leaned against furniture as though they were having trouble waking up. "I'm going to have my juice outside," Ruby said. "Come out."

Daniel followed her onto the front patio in the sun and stood because it felt good to stand. He knew he was an idiot, a slave to the flame, but he couldn't help it.

"Where'd you guys go?" she asked with affected nonchalance.

"To that point over the river."

"Oh! Why didn't you—? Never mind," she cut herself off.

"You weren't alone, Ruby. We figured, you know . . ." and he felt imprisoned by the unsaid, cramped by all the words he had never uttered in Ruby's presence, all seeds of today's bitter harvest.

20.

THE DAY AFTER THE BIG RANCH BARBECUE, Daniel went with Rae to a corn dance at Santo Domingo pueblo. She found him alone down at the barn after breakfast, after he had left Ruby to David on the patio, though Ruby had protested his departure, but he had begged off and said he wanted to get out for a ride alone before he left the ranch. Yet when Rae stopped her car at the barn to check on her mare and its recently weaned foal, Daniel gratefully accepted her invitation to tag along to the Indian ceremony. "I hate to go alone," Rae explained, joining him at the half door to the stall, where he was looking in on the mare and foal. "But Calvin never likes to go to these dances. They make him uncomfortable. Will you come with me? You always liked this sort of thing."

And it was true. He had gone to several pueblo ceremonies with her over the years. So he said, "Sure. I'm ready. Let's go." He followed Rae to the Ford in her Wrangler jeans and jaunty red cowgirl boots, and he couldn't resist saying, because he felt Ruby slipping away, "You've got a pretty sharp-lookin' pair of boots there, Ms. McCullough."

Rae laughed, catching the flirtiness of his tone. "Oh, these ol' things? They're my good luck boots."

But in the car she was quiet, letting him drive and sitting close to the passenger door, watching the landscape roll by.

So it happened that he and Ruby went separately and met by chance, not having planned to converge, but crossing orbits in the shade of the pueblo at the edge of the plaza, surrounded by the unfamiliar syncopated syllables of the Keres language and squat, ageless women looking right through Daniel, not past him or over him or around him, but straight through, as if he had no physical presence, was but a shadow cast in darkness, with Ruby beside him and David wandering up an alley where booths with jewelry had been set up for the few tourists who would stumble upon this timeless ceremony, ageless like the women who looked through Daniel, through the pale alien strangers who would stumble in the brilliant white sunlight, brilliant as silver needles, brightened by the continuous drums, which could be heard even from the parking area across the river, their steady beating not loud but filling the entire village, intimate, throbbing from whichever direction Daniel turned his head to listen. When he finally saw them—large hand-carved wooden cylinders wrapped in stretched rawhide, the men swinging their sticks in controlled strokes—it didn't seem possible they could be so pervasive. He thought they must fill the world, booming away in the background in Santa Fe or Albuquerque as clearly as when he first got out of the car—just as it didn't seem possible they could ever stop or change, while the dancers—hundreds, easily—shuffled along in two lines facing each other, tireless in the heat, moccasins shuffling through the dust, their eyes focused somewhere beyond Daniel's vision.

Rae took it all in, steady and alert, aloof but not detached. Occasionally she would see an acquaintance, an elder she had interviewed perhaps, when she had hoped a living pueblo resident might provide insight into the mute testimony of her Turkey Springs ruin, its crumbled walls as unintelligible to her as the broken rhythms of Keres, which she had once undertaken to study, claiming that she could never know the "Indian mind" without knowing the language; that attempt coming before she decided there was no Indian mind, "The red man is us, and us him," she told Daniel once as he was helping her gather her tools after a day of digging. "He is us a long time ago." So she nodded to this acquaintance but she looked away, as he did, hesitant to inject herself into their ceremony, Daniel thought, better to witness, to watch without commitment.

He watched her watch the dance, while at his side he felt a similar intensity from Ruby, a concentration of the spirit, and a stillness: she quieted herself to watch, and again he felt like a shadow, stretched and flattened and flowing over the terrain, flowing flat over every little bump, flattened against the earth by this brilliant white light, pounded flat by the drums in white light, flattened by her stillness.

So he stood a while with Rae and Ruby, each lost in her own quiet concentration, Daniel suspended between, a shadow watching, until Ruby touched his arm and in that touch released him, the grip of her long fingers around his arm restoring him to a world of three-dimensional wholeness and of desire. She looked up at him, squinting against the sun, and said, "I'm glad you're here. I didn't think I'd see you again before I left," again flattening him, casting him long and thin across the land, as dark as the sun is bright. Her eyes flicked away again to the line of dancers. "Don't you wish you could join in? Or, not join in, but be part of it all. Wake up in the morning in a little room in the pueblo and dress in animal skins. It's so . . . But we can't, can we, Mom?" She raised her voice so Rae would hear.

Rae turned to her, looking past Daniel. "No." She smiled. "I was thinking the very same thing. The very same thing." Her smile broadened.

"This is wild!" David said, having returned from his foray up the alley. He stood beside Daniel with his arms crossed. Daniel looked at him and saw his enjoyment was real, so he nodded and then the drums changed to a new accent, an accelerated polyrhythm, and all the moccasins stepped more rapidly too. David's eyes widened and he laughed, shaking his head in appreciation. Daniel turned back to Rae and saw fine beads of perspiration gathered above her upper lip, then he saw Ruby's eyes on her mother, studying her with the same intensity Rae studied the dance.

"You've never been to one of these before, I take it," Daniel said to David.

"No. What does it all mean?"

"You'd have to ask her," Daniel answered, meaning Rae. The two women stood apart from them, close to each other.

"I'm dying of thirst," David said. "Anyplace we can get a drink of water?"

"I think we passed a stand selling Cokes on the way in."

"It's the real thing," David joked with irony. "You wanna go get one?"

Daniel checked Ruby before answering. In their stillness she and Rae might have been twins. "Sure. They'll never miss us," and it was true, the women didn't even look as he and David turned away and walked back toward the parking area.

"When Ruby said she wanted to come to this thing, I didn't know what she was talking about. She said it was a dance, and I thought, What, like a disco? In the middle of the day? I'm picturing a high school gym, you know? Ruby said she bet you'd be here with her mom."

"Ha!" Daniel replied.

They stopped at a concession stand with a plywood counter nailed to pine poles and roofed with freshly cut, leafy cottonwood branches. In the shade they bought their Cokes from a skinny teenage Indian kid wearing a black Led Zeppelin T-shirt, then they stood to drink them. The boy would occasionally stir a big pot of chile con carne that bubbled over a wood fire. Although the ceremony was hidden from view, the drums still filled the air. From this slightly higher vantage they could see over the roofs of the pueblo houses to the black mesas across the river, wavering in the heat.

"There's nothing like this in LA," Daniel said, pressing the cool wax cup against his forehead.

"I suppose not," Daniel agreed. "Somehow these people have hung on. They threw out the Spanish almost four hundred years ago. Down at Acoma they tossed a priest over the cliff. Rae told me that one. It appeals to her sense of pagan justice."

David laughed and nodded. "There's something pagan about Ruby, don't you think? It's the way she lies out in the sun. One time, I played a gig in a church downtown, and I asked if she wanted to go. She said no, she did all her worshipping on a chaise lounge. Okay, Cleopatra."

"Seems like you two are pretty happy together," Daniel ventured.

David smiled and Daniel felt he had known him a long time, not only for two days of partying at the ranch. "Naw. Well, maybe I am. But Ruby's not happy. Even when she's laughing, having a good time, have you noticed how her eyes are sad, her eyes are crying?"

"I've got to tell you," Daniel began, his ears glowing hot but his tongue thickened by anger, not embarrassment, so he faltered in his confession as he remembered a question Lester had asked him the night before out at the campsite at the Rincón as they sat staring into the piñon fire, dopey from beer, Lester's voice wooden with a strange, almost ritual formality: "Have you ever told her how you really feel about her?" And Daniel had answered "no" right away before regret stole his voice. Lester held him with his eyes and Daniel anticipated the next question before his friend could form the word: "I don't know why." He shook his head and changed tone, first gulping deeply on the warmed flat beer. "I always open the best present last, you know." Lester had stared back, his eyes glinting in the firelight. After a moment, Lester said, "What if it wasn't what you wanted?"

David, his face expectant, waited, and Daniel shook his head. "Never mind. Let's go find the white women."

Giggling and giddy as two teenagers, Rae and Ruby were looking at earrings from one of the jewelry booths. Rae was holding a long silver feather to her lobe, asking, "How do I look?" while Ruby reached for it. "No, it's mine. I saw it first. Daniel, tell Mom to let me buy them!"

"Look." Rae pointed to the table. "There's another pair. Oh! Look at these." She set the first earrings down and picked up a different pair, still attached to the black cardboard carrier, a Hopi-style sand casting of a human hand, palm up, fingers outstretched, like a miniature handprint in the soft sand of a riverbank.

"Just like the carving on the rock at the ranch," Ruby said. "That hand with all the wolves carved around it," but she explained no further to the two men as Rae opened her wallet and counted out twelve one-dollar bills.

"Thank you," Rae told the vendor, and, turning away, put on the new earrings. "There. How do I look? Indian? I'll braid my hair when we get home. Have you ever noticed that the women here"—she gestured to the pueblo women sitting at their booths—"never wear this kind of thing? It's only for the Anglo ladies. Oh, Ruby, you didn't buy the other pair. Do you want to go back?"

"No. I decided not to."

"All the jewelry in the world won't change who we are," Rae said. "It reminds us what we aren't anymore."

The drums boomed closer as they neared the plaza again. "There's a ceremony for everything here," Rae continued as if lecturing. "No one is ever left out. They all get their connection. Connected to the earth, to the whole. They let us come here and watch, I sometimes think, because they know we'll never get it, never see what they see, never know what they know. Just listen to those drums." After they had been quiet a moment, she leaned to Ruby and very maternally said, "I didn't expect to find you here."

"I'm my mother's daughter."

"I guess you are."

"I've got my two men, too. All I need is one more and I'll be exactly like you."

Rae spun away and pushed through the crowd out of sight.

Ruby's smile deepened, exposing more of her lower teeth as if mischief weren't enough, but revenge would do. So Daniel stood by David and Ruby listening to the drums and watching Rae weave away through the ring of onlookers at the plaza, but only Ruby was smiling, her teeth brilliant white needles in a rain of sunlight.

21.

WITH DAVID, RUBY CAME BY TO SEE Daniel at Lester's house in the village above the river on her way back to California. Lester was out back irrigating the garden when Daniel heard them drive up, so he put down his book and went outside to greet them. Ruby seemed carefree and excited and her back was bared by a bright yellow dress. She breezed up to Daniel and touched him as if he were expecting her visit, not resigning himself to a life of occasional hellos and good-byes when she brought her boyfriends to the ranch. Her reappearance in his life that day was like the sudden confused blooming of a rose in February, its brilliant color strange, even unwanted out of season, because it would only awaken premature hope.

Ruby lingered by his side in the shade of the house while David threw a stick for one of the neighbor dogs, and they talked of insignificant things, filling the time with each other before the moment came for her to leave.

"What route are you driving?" Daniel asked.

"Oh, I guess we haven't really decided. We'll probably go over the mountains to I-40, maybe stop for the night in Kingman. It'll be hot so we might try to drive through the desert at night."

"Um-hum," Daniel agreed.

"How long are you going to be here?" she asked.

"Another day or so."

"I wish we could stay longer," Ruby said.

"Where's Lester?" David asked, walking over to them and playing tug-of-war with the dog, which wouldn't let go of the stick.

Daniel nodded toward the garden. "Out back, watering the garden."

"I wanted to tell him good-bye. I enjoyed jamming with him." David walked around the house. Ruby followed, picking her way in sandals through the prickly weeds, Daniel behind her. She stopped at the edge of the tilled area, where three rows of corn had grown almost knee high.

"Hey, there!" Lester greeted them. He stood leaning on his shovel watching the clear water flow from the small acequia into the little channels of the garden. He was barefoot and the mud squished between his toes.

David went over to him. "What are you growing?"

"I'm thirsty," Ruby said low to Daniel. "Can we go inside?"

In the kitchen, Daniel ran her a glass of water at the sink. She drank it down without pause. "The water here always tastes so good," she said, setting the glass down. "Pure."

Still standing by the sink, they looked out the back screen door and saw Lester pointing toward different parts of the garden with the shovel handle, doubtless explaining every part of his budding crop to David, who had taken off his shoes now too.

"I didn't expect you to come by today," Daniel said. "I thought you two would be long gone."

"You sound like you're scolding me."

"No," he said. "I've got no right to do that. That's your mom's department."

"I stayed up half of last night talking to her," she answered. "It was so nice. We haven't talked that way for so long. I think I convinced her to come out and visit me. What about you? You said you might."

"Sheeesh!" he exclaimed, his voice sharp with anger.

"What!"

"Why do you do this?" he asked.

"Do what?"

Daniel waved his arm toward David in the garden. "Who's he, your butler?" He stepped away from her but couldn't think where to go, not while there was still a chance of having her. "Do you get some perverse pleasure out of playing red light, green light with me?" He felt he was yelling.

"At least David's not afraid of me."

"You think I'm afraid? Of what?" he demanded. She didn't reply and into the silence an answer presented itself: to let her be real.

She turned away from him, her back brown and smooth and rippled with light muscling like a streambed of water-carved sand. "I wanted to see you, that's why I came by." Her hand dropped to the counter, fingers sliding along the metal flashing as if it could be read, a tactile oracle that revealed the solution to some recurring problem. Her hand fell to her side. "I miss you, Daniel. I'm sorry."

Silenced by a confusion of anger and pride and loneliness, he waited for her to continue, but she remained quiet. "Sorry for what?" he asked.

"For not being ready. That's what I wanted to tell you."

She paced toward the door, then back toward him, then turning to look outside again. "Look at Lester. He looks like somebody from the Bible. That's what I said to Mom last night, that's why she likes him. Loves him. Boy, is that hard to say: my mother's lover. I suppose she deserves a little happiness. You know, I hardly said two words to Dad the whole time I was here. We avoided each other, and sometimes he would see me talking to Lester, like at the barbecue, and he looked so sad, like Mom and I had both betrayed him. And really, he's the one who did the betraying. Worse than that. But he's known about them for years. Years. I start feeling like I'm part of the conspiracy. And I wonder, how can he know, for so long, and keep right on working with Lester? But then, I know all about keeping secrets. Do you think they ever talk about it, about her?"

"You can work all day with those two guys and never hear a complete sentence anyhow," Daniel answered, accepting her digression as a truce. "But you're right, it's strange. You know, I think they really like each other, still. It's like Calvin doesn't hold it against Lester. It's something they have between them, something in common."

"That's twisted, Daniel."

"Yeah, well," he allowed, thinking about the camaraderie he had felt with David at the pueblo the day before. "Women make us do strange things."

"Like it's *our* fault?" she protested. "That's bullshit!"

"You sound like Rae."

"Maybe we shouldn't talk," Ruby said, and she sat down at the kitchen table. "I'm sorry I'm giving you such a hard time."

"Stop apologizing, Rube."

"When you first came to the ranch, you seemed older, and all grown up." Her eyes flipped up to him, dark and dangerous, her tongue tapping her teeth. "It's really only recently I realized I could hurt you."

22.

"DO YOU WANT TO GO BACK?" Daniel asks. They still sit close together on the mesa top but he senses her thoughts have fled far away.

Ruby seems to consider his question for a moment, then returns obliquely: "Tell me this: do you really believe Dad didn't bury Mom? Do you really believe he brought her out here?"

"It's what Lester told me. He helped Calvin load . . . He helped Calvin with it, but he didn't go along."

"He hasn't actually told me he did it," Ruby says. "I just feel it. And I asked Lester, and he right away denied it, so I knew he was lying. But I had a dream a few nights ago—I've had a hundred dreams. . . . In one of them, I was walking up here with her, like when we used to take hikes, but she was sitting under this big tree, leaning up against it, and she was saying"—again her voice tightens and her eyes fill—"you'll always know where to find me." She puts her hand quickly to her eyes. "You'll always know where to find me. And the tree was right over there, up in there." She gestures toward where she had been walking. "I thought I might find . . . something. But there aren't any tracks, or anything. It's a wild-goose chase." She looks west now to the opposing cliff that forms the other half of Mesa Reina across Water Canyon from them. "There's one more place. Over there. But I don't think we have time now. Maybe tomorrow."

"Does it really matter where—"

"Of course it does! It matters."

They are riding again and Ruby settles into a preoccupied silence. He lets his faster-gaited horse build up a long lead, and only occasionally he checks over his shoulder to see that she's still following.

Harvey comes riding up the trail.

"Lester told me where I'd find you," he says, not looking at either of them as Ruby catches up and reins in her horse. He dismounts and rubs his horse's sweaty face. "Still pretty warm for October." Harvey keeps his attention focused on the horse. "Ruby, I wanted to tell you, it's not what you think. Last night Dad just wanted to go out to the house and see it."

"He was looking for evidence. He's going to destroy some of it and use the rest for himself."

"But what for? It doesn't make any sense."

"The will. Come on, Harv. You know. She rewrote it last summer. He's going to challenge her 'mental state,' or something like that. And it's not just that. He's got to get to the journals first so he can sort through them, or he's busted. He'll be exposed and everyone will know I'm telling the truth. He's looking for a reason to excuse his behavior."

"About what?"

"Never mind." Ruby glances at Daniel.

"Come on, Ruby, let's not get on different sides of this thing. You and I have always been able to talk. Dad's not after our inheritance. He knows the ranch is really his, that he'll still run it."

Ruby's face is stern, unyielding, her head slowly shaking from side to side. "I don't care about the ranch. I care about the truth. About telling the truth."

But Harvey interrupts. "Everything was fine! Wasn't everything going fine now, really? I mean, Mom and Dad had differences, sure, and you . . . but—" and Harvey looks to Ruby, an anguished plea contorting his features, as if she were his only hope for some final reconciliation, but her face stays hard, smooth and opaque, an expression uncannily like Rae might have looked at twenty when confronted by one of the world's insatiable demands, and Daniel thinks of angels, and of doors swinging open on broken hinges so that spirits are free to pass, free to roam not only night, but the daylight world.

"And there's one other thing," Ruby continues, turning to Daniel, her voice leveling off. "Tomás is my real father. Like that wasn't always totally obvious."

"You're kidding!" Daniel erupts, but an icy hollow shudder spreads through his gut like a body knowledge that says, "Of course. I knew it all along." Obviously Harvey knows. Probably Lester too, Daniel realizes.

But Ruby isn't waiting for Daniel to process this new fact. "It was Tomás who made Dad bury her on some mesa top. He and Lester knew that's what she wanted."

Harvey stares down at his boots, tears running off his face, and he takes a deep breath, mustering strength to ask, "Did you find where . . . ?"

"No!"

"Maybe it isn't true, then. Maybe he packed her into the funeral home like he said he was going to."

"No," Ruby says. "He wanted to control all of this."

"But even Lester wasn't there to see what happened."

"It's true." Ruby sighs, her anger and distress melting into a shapeless state. Daniel sees her body settle after she takes her feet out of the stirrups to stretch. "It's all like a dream, isn't it? I've always heard people say that about a crisis like this. We've just got to get used to it, Harv," and now her eyes are soft as they settle on her brother. "Let's go home."

When she sets her feet into the stirrups again, she twists a bit to look back toward the point of the mesa above them to the east, where a faint sliver of moon winks from beyond the planet's smooth sphere.

23.

AFTER THEY HAVE UNSADDLED THE HORSES and eaten lunch, she insists on driving to the Turkey Springs ranch: she wants to see where her mother died and look for the journals herself. Tomás and Calvin are nowhere around, their horses still gone. Lester's car is gone too.

"Are you sure?" Daniel asks.

"Yes! I'm going. Look, her journals were out there. And she kept the older ones in a strongbox, stashed someplace. She was weird about them and I know she would have put them somewhere safe. And her will must be with them."

Ruby drives the Scout because it will be muddy in spots, and the highway stretch passes quickly, a few quick miles on the wide, new road. Ruby's attention again and again wanders north toward the cliffs. Ahead, to the west, a low bank of clouds is coasting in over Mesa de San Francisco and Daniel wonders if the weather will again turn wet and cold.

"Are you all right?" he asks.

"Yes."

"Just checking."

"Okay," and she puts her hand on his leg. "Thanks. I love you. Did I tell you that? Oh, Daniel, it's so absurd. Since I was maybe fifteen, it's always been you. Every other guy I ever went out with, I was always looking for you in him. I'm so stupid."

"Hey, I'm not that bad. . . ."

"No, I mean for waiting."

"I know."

Ruby makes the turn onto the ranch road to the Turkey Springs homestead a dozen miles up the river canyon. She stops and he hops out to lock the front hubs, then she shifts to four-wheel drive. The road starts up a narrow little canyon, hardly more than an arroyo, then climbs to run across a broad bench, and here the mud is axle deep. Ruby powers through, water and mud spraying up onto the windshield so she has to keep the wipers on, and Daniel braces against the dashboard. He loves that she can drive this way. They slew across the boggy stretch. After a mile or so, the road drops off the plateau and follows the river, immediately below the western scarp that borders the flats.

"Remember we all used to go camping here?" Daniel asks.

"Of course. When I was little, that was my favorite thing to do. It was really pretty nice of you guys to let me tag along. I hope I wasn't a pain."

"Oh, no. God, Ruby, when you were fifteen, you looked like nineteen. You drove me crazy."

"Really?"

"Are you kidding? You didn't know?"

"No. Well, I suppose—"

"Yeah. Lester and I were out here last spring. I was up for a visit and some of the cattlemen were driving their herds across your pastures up into the high country, and we were supposed to help them out—and, really, keep them from mixing any McCullough cows into their herds. So we camped out, and in the morning we sat up on the point, each of us with a pair of binoculars, and watched cattle go by—and go by and go by. Jesus, what a day."

"Oh, I bet you loved it."

"Naturally."

But first Daniel and Lester had awakened in dew-dampened sleeping bags to watch the sun bob above the mountains amid broad waves of color, rising to burn away any dampness from the desert, one of those transcendent, absurdly full late-spring days when the spirit of the place, all that slumbering mirac-ulous power overflowed in the dense, palpable smell of sage and the fine dust and the rounded sandstone cliffs warding ancient bones, that power seeping into him like the fine alkali that leaches into the river-valley fields, forced upward by the unseen hydraulics of groundwater.

Daniel built a small cook fire, starting with strips of juni-per bark, then twigs and bigger branches and finally laying a piñon log on top, then nestling the coffeepot on one edge and setting the frying pan into the coals, while Lester peeled off strips of bacon and chopped up an onion for the omelet, and Lester said, "You know, don't you, that Rae and I are, uh, still sleeping together." His blond hair, long past his shoulders, hid most of his face as he bent to the task of cooking.

"Yeah, I know."

"Um." He diced more onion and scraped it into the pan, now greasy with bacon fat. "I've never known anyone like her. I guess I ought to feel guilty, but I don't. Shit, Calvin knows. It's almost like it relieves him, somehow. We're still good friends. I can't fucking believe that, really, but you know I work with him all the time. We talk about the ranch, and the kids and how they're doing and all. But Rae is in tune with things. One time

I was out hiking with her above Turkey Springs, and we'd been out for a while, and it was pretty chilly, let me tell you, and I was all for heading home, so we're truckin' along the top of the cliffs above that old road—remember, where we found that rusty old lantern?—and then she stopped and said she wanted to climb down, I mean, we're talking rock climbing here. So I go over with her and we look down and it looks impossible, without ropes and equipment, and maybe some skill, which I don't have. I said, 'No friggin' way am I goin' down here.' But she said, 'No, there's a way down here. They used to come up and down right here.' And she kind of walked back and forth on the top a few times, then she said, 'There,' and I looked and there were these carved-out stairs in the rock, like a ladder. She said she'd never been there before. They went right down to the bottom. So then she said there must be a site around somewhere, and we split up and walked around in the trees and pretty soon she found the walls and a few shards and that was how she found the first Turkey Springs site—arrow shafts even, and a couple skeletons. But when she found those stairs, I couldn't see anything until she showed me. Even looking for them, I couldn't see where they started—you can't see them from the top, and down below you're in the trees so you can't see up that part of the cliff."

He paused, maybe seeing it all again. "And sometimes, she reads my mind. Absolutely. Or she'll know something about my childhood even, for chrissake, some little thing that happened when I was ten, that I know I never told anybody about." He looked at Daniel then, closely, that unwavering blue-eyed stare, unblinking. "I can't say 'no' to her. I did at first, actually. I couldn't really believe she was coming on to me. But one time when Calvin was gone to visit his dad a couple days at the rest home down in Albuquerque, she had me over to the house and that was it. This was a couple years ago."

The road winds about ten feet above the river, curving and dipping across small tributary arroyos and sometimes turning sharply around a boulder that's fallen from the cliffs or a ponderosa too big and too old for Calvin to have cut down when he bulldozed the road in. Before he bladed it, there had only been a jeep trail here, and a cowhand working for the ranch had often been stranded at the Turkey Springs cabin for days at a time by snow or mud when it thawed. Daniel had once helped Calvin clear the road after a heavy cloudburst washed out one of the culverts, and the sight and sound of the Caterpillar laboring away amid all that vast empty country, dwarfed to the size of a toy by the mesas and the huge rocks along the river, made the work seem a petty, foolish struggle against overwhelming elemental forces. When they took a lunch break and the diesel was shut off, the silence was astounding: he felt he could hear the sun sliding along its track across the sky, but Calvin chewed his sandwich as if there were no contradictions, no unsolvable puzzles or clueless mysteries.

Ruby drives slowly enough that he can look all around, studying the canyon walls so close on either side and the cottonwoods brilliant yellow along the banks, each leaf gently aflutter in some tiny breeze running downstream over the water. Ruby too seems alive to the place, and she points once when they drive close to the river as a blue heron lifts so slowly and stately from the water and skims across to alight in a tree on the far bank.

"I saw my first bald eagle here," Daniel says. "In the winter, February," and it was so huge and snowy-white headed that his eyes misted over and he almost didn't see the second one, high, high up in the sky so he could barely distinguish its markings. Both birds stroked steadily up the canyon and soon were lost from sight.

Now the road takes a sharp turn. Ruby nearly stops to negotiate the bend. Set into the red sand embankment on the outside of the curve is a cross of carefully placed river rocks, each chosen for its smooth roundness. All around, the slanting sand has been raked and picked clean of twigs and pebbles. The embankment tilts at a forty-five-degree angle and the entire image is no bigger than the bed of a pickup truck.

"Oh, look!" Ruby says, and she is already opening her door to get out. He follows her and she crouches down low to run her hand over the bottom few stones. The heavy clouds have held off to the north, leaving the canyon in sunshine.

"I haven't seen this before," Ruby gasps. "Who did it?" She keeps her hand on the rock, which gleams white in the sunshine.

"Lester," Daniel replies. "Didn't you know? For devotion, he told me. And as a gift to your mom."

Ruby stands and pulls him to her. She stretches to his face and closes her eyes and kisses him and her tongue lightly flicks into his mouth. "Do you want me?"

She takes his hand and leads him across the road and down a small slope to the bank of the river, where a cluster of oaks and willows hides a broad bed of flattened grass tramped down on the sand by sleeping deer or elk. The river is muddy and wide and swift but unbroken. Ruby sits with her legs folded under her and gently tugs him down to the ground and they kiss again while his hands find the bottom hem of her sweatshirt and slide inside it, up the rippling skin over her ribs, then the weightier fullness of her breasts and she hums in his ear. He pulls the shirt up and off and her hair is wild with static as her hands find his belt, undoing his pants button by button and reaching in, her touch cool, delicate, subtle like the digital leaves of willows wavering in the breeze. She tugs off his clothes, pushing him to lie down and—half undressed herself—hovering above him, her hair tickling his face when she again sets her lips to his, drawing at him as if she might slake once and for all an ancient thirst. Her skin is hot and soft, her body malleable in his hands, the tips of her breasts dragging across his chest as she keeps herself slightly above him.

"Cold?" he asks, whispering.

She shakes her head and says, "Shhh . . ." to hush him. He lies flat on his back and she kneels straddling him, leaning onto her hands, her arms to either side, and now he fumbles with her cowgirl jeans, the zipper, that unthinkably satin skin, surprisingly white where it hasn't sunned. Ruby stands to step out of the clothing and he sits up, nuzzling his way up her thigh, delirious, because he had come to think this never would happen, he would never ask, and now he swirls in disbelief, every sense heightened by the scent at the base of her neck, the shallow sound of her breath, the guiding strength of her arms as she lies back and pulls him onto her, her legs opening for him with the sweetest of all invitations. She smiles, her teeth glistening in the sunlight, her eyes wise as he slides in.

As he penetrates her, all his feelings center on that point of entry. He is overtaken by rhythm. The thought comes that he is measuring a half foot of darkness. He forces her hips tighter to him and she winces and then it's over. Seeing he is done, her eyes settle on him flat, wary, as lucid as noon. From the ache of wanting her, he drops into an ear-ringing wake of nothing, the hollow void abandoned by fleeting desire. Into that vacuum the nature of love demands a choice from him, an act of intention either toward her or away, back into himself. He knows she has long ago discovered this emptiness, this disappointed wisdom like a deer trail suddenly split into two parts, one climbing up among the cliffs toward the sky through a maze of cracks and chimneys of sandstone, the other along their base, circling back whence it came. He fears he can't offer the love she needs, and she can't provide the wisdom he seeks. The choice waits.

He dreads she might speak.

"That's it," she says. "That's all I've got." She gently but insistently shoves him off, then curls her body away from his.

Echoing how he felt ten minutes ago he says, "It's enough," before realizing it's the wrong thing. On the downhill path now, he can do nothing but stumble forward. "You don't know how much I want you. I've always wanted you. I always will."

"My mother didn't want me," she spits out, and he realizes she's crying. "But my father sure as shit wanted me—for one thing."

They lie in silence a moment as Ruby's words rattle around in Daniel's head looking for a place to land. Despite the *aha!* he can't quite process them now. The atmosphere around them sags like an old balloon, emptied of all the tension and purpose that inflated the last five minutes. Blank and limp as damp paper, Daniel waits.

"You don't want me, not all of me, not the ugly part. You thought you did, but I'm the broken Christmas present."

"It doesn't seem like it was the right time to do this, I guess. We should have waited. I'm sorry. Now you know I'm like every other guy."

Ruby sits up and gathers her sweatshirt over her slumped shoulders and he notices her breasts droop toward her stomach and a wave of shame further numbs his thoughts: mentally he's got nowhere to go.

"I just wanted you to hold me, really," she says, her voice sad but stabilizing, her back to him as she gets dressed. "So I asked the one way I know for sure gets results. At least I knew

I had your attention. It's not your fault. I knew what I was doing. I'm good at it."

Ruby stands and wipes her eyes dry with the long edge of her index finger so she won't smear her makeup. Daniel gets up and buttons his Levi's. They hear a cow insistently lowing from the willows on the far bank of the river. He steps behind Ruby and wonders if he should hold her, wonders if in the absence of wanting her he still likes her or even himself.

As he starts to speak, to declare like an incantation against darkness that he must love her, with familiar clairvoyance she says, "Don't promise me anything right now. You won't mean it. I'm not who you think I am. Now that Mom's dead, I don't suppose I'm who I think I am. My roof fell in, the walls are tipping. . . . I have to complete what I came back to do. Act like you're my friend and we'll take it from there."

"I can do that."

"I've let you see too much of me." She sighs.

"Nothing's changed, Rube. . . ." He trails off, wondering if he could survive a future that replicates their past.

"Nothing, except now we've done it, " she disagrees, "and there's not even that ahead of us. Now there's nothing left to pretend."

Somehow they wrap themselves in old habits of conversation and are able to continue the drive, but this new thing between them won't stay covered. She settles against her door and keeps her eyes on her driving. He had liked it better when she chatted and his left leg sprawled toward the middle so her hand bumped his knee when she shifted into high gear.

"Why didn't you ever call me in California?" she asks.

"I dreamed about you," he answers. "And I even tried to

call you once, but David answered, and I hung up. I never told you that. . . ."

"You did?" she says, surprised, turning to look at him. "Why did you hang up?"

"It was too much, having him answer—"

"Oh, brother!" She looks away out the window. "I slept with David only a few times, when we first met, and he seemed so—I don't know what it was. But then it was like we were happier together when we didn't have sex. We even slept together, without fucking. Mom didn't believe me when I told her, when he came with me for the barbecue. It was companionship. He really likes me."

"So do you think it was a mistake, what we did back there just now?" he asks.

"Do you?" she returns. "What do you think, Daniel? It's not all up to me, you know, none of this. Not Mom and Dad, not Lester, not you." She measures her words carefully. "Stop pretending you're not part of everything. You're responsible too. For what you do and for what you don't do. You could have fucked me a couple years ago, you know."

"I didn't know," he protests. "You put me off."

"You didn't really want to," she corrects him.

"I suppose. You looked so good up on that pedestal."

"I'm not in love with him, exactly," Ruby says now, after riding a few slow miles in layered silence. She has moved past the opacity of anger to a more refractive musing. She weaves the truck through the yellow-leafed cottonwoods alongside Turkey Spring, which here is an intermittent stream, the water flowing for a hundred yards, then vanishing into the sand and reappearing again farther down the arroyo. "But I trust him. I think he genuinely likes me. Sometimes I sing with him while he plays. I've never sung with anybody before. I love him, I suppose, in some way. He's a really decent guy. When they stopped playing that night, the Fourth, and you sort of walked away, I felt like crying, like you'd finally, totally given up on me. Here I'd just had this long, long talk with Mom, and we talked about you, and I thought, what if I never see you again? That seems so long ago—only three months. And now I know what that really means, not to see someone again."

"I figured, after the barbecue, after seeing you with David, that I had to learn to live without you," he says. "I'd always hoped that somehow, someday, we'd hook up, but you gave me such mixed signals that night, and I knew you cared about me, but shit! there you were with this other guy, and he seemed like a helluva guy, too. And I thought, why am I dying this slow death over you?" He hears the anger in his words, an old mute resentment suddenly finding voice.

24.

RUBY ROLLS THE TRUCK TO A STOP in front of the gate that separates pasture from the Turkey Springs homestead.

"Are you sure you want to see the house?" he asks, thinking: Ashes. He looks out the window at the metal farm gate because he cannot bear the grief in her face.

"I have to," she says.

When he gets out of the car to open the gate, he sees tire tracks in the damp sand, then he remembers that the other men had driven here last night, so he undoes the chain without further concern, she drives the Scout through, then Daniel latches the gate shut again. Though the house site isn't yet visible, he catches a faint, smothering smell of damp charcoal drifting on the air and he glances at Ruby, who looks straight ahead as if they are approaching a precipice.

"I'm going to sit here a minute?" Ruby says, hand on the gearshift.

"Okay. How about we turn around and we go back to the house. Let's go to Santa Fe, stay at La Fonda, just for tonight, so you can get a little air from all this?"

"No." The sun slips behind a cloud and Ruby looks pale, her eyes dull, her body's energy discharged. "Maybe tomorrow.

Or the next day. We all have to meet with the lawyer tomorrow afternoon in Santa Fe."

"Are you expecting to find something here?" he asks. She nods but makes no move to get out.

"I'll go," he concludes.

Most of the house is gone, and what remains is charred, collapsed, caved in. The outbuildings—barn, loafing shed, another small dwelling—still stand, but the shed looks dried, heat-blasted, singed. Ruby stays in the truck while Daniel walks around the ruin, then spots Lester's car behind the barn but no sign of the man. Daniel pokes around the buildings a minute, then notices boot tracks heading along the path up the canyon toward the dig.

Back at the Scout he tells Ruby what he has seen. She nods as if this were expected. "He'll get them, then."

"The journals?"

She nods quickly, sniffling and wiping at her nose with a Kleenex.

"Should we catch up to him?" Daniel begins, but she shakes her head no.

"It's all right. Lester loved her," Ruby whispers. "He'll give them to me."

"Where are they?"

"At the site." Her voice strengthens. "In the underground chamber, I think. I had this dream last week, before . . . everything: Mom was taking me around the dig, explaining all about it like I'd never seen it before, and I guess in the dream I hadn't. When we came to the chamber I helped her drag the big stone to the side and she was saying, 'This is where they kept their seeds, in metal jars,' which of course didn't make any sense, but when we moved the stone, I heard chanting coming out. . . . I couldn't understand it, but Mom said, 'Listen to the words, Ruby. They tell the whole story.' She looked beautiful and happy in the dream. She seemed so calm. We sat there a while, listening to this strange language. There might have been drums, even, I don't remember. Then she held me close and it was like I was little again—I guess she was saying good-bye."

Daniel leans against the Scout's fender beside Ruby's open window. Above, the sky is half blue, but a clean edge of clouds is sliding over the mesas from the northwest, blotting the sun and chilling the air. He watches a hawk soar around the western cliffs while two swallows dive to peck at it. The hawk banks a tight turn and flutters onto the tip of a pine tree. There is no wind and for a moment the canyon is absolutely silent, the golden-leafed trees not stirring.

Ruby opens her door and gets out, tugging at her sweatshirt and smoothing her clothes and looking around as if she were in a strange new place and frightened.

"Maybe we should go find Les," Daniel suggests. "Could be he needs help."

"You go ahead," Ruby says, turning away from him, her shoulders hunched, her arms clenched around her breast as if a frigid wind were blowing up the canyon.

He follows Lester's tracks up the dry riverbed; they turn onto the trail through the four-wing saltbush and chamisa and sage, leading across a meadow to the site, the first ruin Rae found in this canyon, apparently a few mere lumps of dirt in a brief meadow overlooking the wash, until she began digging, and walls emerged, houses, pots, hand tools, mummified corncobs, and broken beams of ponderosa pine; then the strange underground chamber and whatever weird magic it released.

"Was that it?" Daniel asks as he approaches Lester, who

surely has heard him coming but remains still, sitting on a low wall, his arms resting on his knees, his hands together but only the fingertips touching, a pose of delicate reflection. "She opened that thing up and then came unglued?"

Lester shakes his head. Before him the rock slab has been pulled away and the dark hole stands revealed but unilluminated. "How can you say?" Lester returns, still staring at his fingers. "Can you really set a time to it? Maybe some event triggered it, tripped her up for that final fall. I don't know. I can't figure it." Daniel stops and sets a foot up on the stone wall to rest. "I know she was really coming to terms with her past, what happened with Calvin and Ruby. Admitting it all to herself, writing about it in her journals." Lester nods toward the hole. "Yeah, they're in there. I put 'em there with Rae a few weeks ago. That should have told me something was up with her. Anyway, I was gonna get 'em and give 'em to Ruby. I figure they're hers now. I can't see givin' them to Calvin, not the way he's feeling. That's why I wanted to get here first. Sorry I didn't tell you. I wanted some time alone. . . ."

"It's cool," Daniel says softly.

"Where's Ruby?"

"Back there." He nods down the canyon.

"Um." Lester looks up at him, those deep blue eyes drilling in for a moment, then flipping away, scanning the cliff tops, the trees. "She—Rae—told me she sometimes thought of killing herself. She said she couldn't stand the guilt. She once told me she had insight but not wisdom—seeing but not knowing. Isn't that funny? Calvin and me talked about that a little bit yesterday, how sometimes it seemed like she had this total awareness, but she never gained anything from it. I think she understood the darkness in him but lacked the courage to act against him. She lived in darkness, that's for sure. And she always wanted Ruby to be pure, pure, pure. Untainted. A virgin in white. And of course Calvin fixed that. But it was never a big deal about Harvey. He doesn't have that—awareness—not like Ruby. If you turn it on yourself, it eats you. That's what happened to Rae. Just ate out her mind.

"You know, she started with me, she picked me up on the highway that day to irritate Calvin. Yeah, that's how she looked at it. She told me. She said she knew it would bug him. She said she was always looking for ways to avoid loving him, to avoid really opening up to him, giving up something to him. Some kind of power... She once told me," and Lester laughs, short, barely a chuckle, "she told me once that Eve's mistake wasn't eating the apple. It was giving Adam a piece. She gave it away. . . . And it was after I came that he started messing with Ruby."

"Jesus." Daniel sits down next to Lester on the low wall of the pueblo ruin.

"Remember how Ruby used to come out to the bunk-house?" Daniel says to Lester. "I remember once she asked me if I thought she was adopted, because she couldn't believe they were really her parents. She focused it all on Rae. 'Only a stepmother can be so mean.' God, even back then, they looked so much alike."

"But it was really Calvin who was fucking her up. And the weird thing is, Rae seemed to hold that against Ruby. Ruby was so sexy, and it ate Rae up," Lester says. "And Ruby always knew how to turn the knife and get that little extra bit of hurt."

"And she's paying for it now," Daniel says, meeting Lester's eyes again, and Lester nods slowly. "But what do you mean Calvin—"

Lester looks off. "That's not for me to tell. The funny thing is, to me Rae was the most generous person in the world,"

Lester says. "She'd do anything. Just to have me around. I never knew anyone like that."

"She never gave Ruby a break," Daniel says.

"No. I know."

Over their heads, the line of clouds continues to flow slowly southeast.

"I try to imagine this place alive, with people, doing whatever it was they did, you know?" Lester says. "Rae could do that, I think. She could actually see it, see them. She could see the whole pueblo standing, and women sitting in the shade grinding corn and the men maybe dragging a deer carcass across the little plaza. She had visions."

"Like Ruby."

"Does she?"

"Yeah."

They are quiet a while, then Daniel nods toward the hole and says, "Have you brought the journals out?"

"No. I checked they were still there. In a way, I don't really want to. I'd just as soon leave 'em buried. It's funny: they explain a lot, but there's really no one left to explain it all to."

Then Daniel feels her behind him, feels the pressure of her eyes on the back of his head, and he turns and Ruby is standing on a small rise in the trail, looking down on them, her arms folded across her chest in that pose of willed containment, as if she might hold it all in forever and not blow apart and scatter across the earth like autumn leaves. Her face is dark, haggard, her mouth open slightly. She breathes quickly from walking. They look at each other a moment. Beside him, Daniel feels Lester grow still, though he has not turned to follow Daniel's gaze.

Far enough away that she has to raise her voice, Ruby says, "Are they there?" In the slight breeze now coming down the canyon, her words are muffled and small, snatched away almost before reaching him.

Lester turns then and says, "Yeah."

Ruby comes down, goes to the hole, kneels, and reaches in. Daniel hears the tinny sound of metal as the box scrapes against earth and it emerges in her hands, apparently heavy, clumphing to the ground. Daniel and Lester remain sitting while Ruby runs her fingers along the edges of the strongbox, which seems far too small to hold a lifetime of diaries and a legal will.

"There," she whispers, sitting back on her heels but keeping her fingertips on the beige metal. She looks at the two men. "Don't tell Dad?"

"Okay," Lester says, and Daniel nods too.

Ruby opens the box, runs her hand over the stack of small notebooks. She takes out a folded legal document—the will. "There's only one thing I need to know, really. I think she said where she wanted to be buried. I think she planned all this and she would have written about it." Ruby checks Lester and he shrugs. "But now I think I know where she is anyhow," Ruby continues. "There's only one place it could be."

"Where, Ruby?" Lester asks.

"Up there. There's another spot above Water Canyon. You can drive down to it from Cañoncito if you know the way. I should have thought of that today. Where else could it be?"

"Do you want to go?" Lester asks her.

"No. Not now. Tomorrow. I'm sure that's the place. Somewhere up there. Above the ruins. We can find out here." She gestures at the strongbox of journals.

"To drive we have to go all the way around on the highway," Daniel says, his mind tracing over the various routes on this renewed hunt. "It's too late, too far to hike it. If we had horses . . . Either way, we'd be lucky to get up there today. And if it snows, or rains . . ."

"I know!" she says, her fingers still on the box. "I want to talk to Dad. Let's go home."

Daniel looks at Lester, who says, "Go ahead. I'm gonna stay a while. I might even camp. I dunno."

Ruby's eyes narrow on Lester in evident disapproval, but she does not speak.

25.

"CAN YOU BELIEVE THIS WEATHER?" Tomás is saying, a Coors in one hand and a sandwich in the other. They have all gathered in the kitchen, picking ham off the platter—last night's leftovers—and spooning piles of potato salad onto their plates. Tomás seems relieved, almost light-hearted. "Yesterday it snows. Today it's warm like summer. Then another one of these little fronts blows in and its winter again. There's no 'counting for it, eh, Calvin?"

Calvin looks at him and nods, his mouth full, his hair pressed flat in a ring from wearing his hat all day, his eyes still gleaming with a strange elation. Harvey looks to Calvin too, looks up from his chair, a deep glass of whiskey on the table in front of him. He is drinking seriously now, steadily and purposefully and without regard for his father's disapproval.

"It's going to be a snowy winter, *qué no*, Calvin?" Tomás continues. "Look at the horses, they started growing long coats two weeks ago, barely October." He takes a deep pull on his Coors, and when he lowers the bottle his lips glisten till he wipes them with the back of his hand.

"I don't know," Calvin replies, his eyes now fixed on blank space between the refrigerator and Ruby, who is pulling apart a head of lettuce for sandwiches, her long fingers working quickly as they separate the leaves and then pass them beneath running water to wash, and she says to Daniel, "I don't know how much longer this lettuce will be good. It's a little brown around the edges," her words passing under Calvin's and pitched only to Daniel's ears.

"I think it's too early to tell." Calvin addresses the blank space. "You never can tell."

Tomás nods and continues to eat.

Ruby pats the lettuce leaves with a paper towel, then turns to him, her face flushed. "Let's get out of here!" She ducks her head and slips around Tomás, disappears through the door-way. They hear the outside screen door slam.

"I guess I should go have a talk with that girl," Calvin tells the space by the refrigerator. He doesn't move.

Daniel is the one to follow her, and he finds she has not fled far; she stands a step or two outside the carport, composed and quiet in the dark.

"What star is that?" Daniel asks, raising a shadowy hand to the west, where a point of light shines through a gap in the clouds. "It's the evening star, isn't it?"

"Venus," Ruby says.

He moves beside her, no longer concerned about touching. It doesn't seem to matter. "I thought so. What would we see, if we had a telescope?" Daniel knows she knows these things because Rae would have taught her.

"It would be white, and round, or three-quarter round, like the moon. Venus goes through phases, like the moon, from full to half to—"

"How female," Daniel interrupts. "You women have these cycles, these cosmic cycles, right inside. Is it an advantage?"

"You tell me. It's like we're all in some strange orbit around some invisible sun. Sometimes the light's shining on us, then sometimes we're on the dark side." She pauses and he moves closer so their bodies almost touch. "Where does that leave you, I wonder. What about men?"

"That's easy," he says. "We go round and round you. You're the center."

"All of us?"

"No. One at a time."

"It's what happened to Dad." Her tone has changed now, taken on years, weathered and bleached to a shiny smoothness. "He lost his center. I think that's what happens: you—men— you put it into us, don't you? Like Adam, the rib, something taken out of you that keeps pulling you toward us. Sometimes that force is too much and you give in and forget everything else." Still with that dry, polished tone to her voice, she says, "I keep getting stranger. And I wonder if I'll wake up one day and find I've stepped over the edge. Or maybe it's not that obvious, but instead you get more and more drawn into this one way of thinking and being, and then you can't remember thinking and being any other way. You're out there on your own, no way back. Mom isolated herself that way. At first it was a mental thing, in her head, spiritual. Maybe it started when she abandoned me to him, blamed me. Then moving out to Turkey Springs was the next logical step."

The night is too cold, too dark, so Daniel says, "You can step out of it. Something snaps and you're outside. You don't think that way anymore."

"You think so?"

"I guess," he replies, still looking at that lifeless planet above the horizon. "What do you want to do now?"

"I can't go back in there." Ruby pulls away from him and steps deeper into the night. "I used to be so afraid of the dark, when I was five or six. Just terrified. Nothing specific. Pure, absolute terror, like you only feel in a really good nightmare—so afraid, you can't even think. But here, now, this darkness—nothing could feel safer. It's like being held." She takes a few more aimless steps away from him, away from the house and the light of the windows. All he can see of her is a vague form, darkness on darkness. Her movements are indistinct. If he does not look directly at her, but averts his eyes slightly and lets her image strike the edges of his retina, she sharpens, the lines of her form take on a more comforting firmness—by not looking, he sees.

"We could make love here," she is saying, "twenty feet from the house, beyond where that light from the bathroom falls, and no one would know we were even here. We might as well be a million miles out there." Her gesture draws his direct gaze, and the arm seems to vanish as he tries to focus, so he lets his eyes drift, and her silhouette condenses again in his peripheral vision. It is a strange trick of the eyes, and he continues to experiment, looking toward the voice, the movement, then looking away again.

"We could make love across the arroyo, and it would be like there was no one else anywhere in the world." Her voice is detached; it seems to float in space, to be space, and it gives him the sensation of overhearing her thoughts: against this disintegration of barriers, he says, "Do you want to make love?"

"No," she whispers, a syllable blended with the cold breeze that now speaks through the oak leaves and willows. "Yes," she amends, but with a new caprice in her voice. She has moved farther away. "Right here." He walks toward her. "But you wouldn't. You'd be afraid, Daniel. What if Dad came out? Or Lester. I almost did it with him once, you know." He stands near her again. "Of course you know. You guys talk about everything." He can't see them, but he imagines her teeth, her tongue flicking across them to whet the tease. "I'm a good lay, aren't I. It used to be one of my goals in life. Lester was sort of an experiment for me. I really wanted to hurt you that time. And Mom too, I wanted to get to her. I could take the men away from her. That was always my highest card, my best weapon—I wanted you to come back, to sweep me away, to care for me: you were gone. So I spent the night with Lester, I offered myself to him, and I cried my little eyes out."

"Ruby, I'm here now." He holds her shoulders.

"Are you?" she asks, as if she can sense the shift within him that began this afternoon by the river. "I think it's too late."

"It doesn't have to be," he answers, struggling with the words as if this dark night cloaked his thoughts, hid away the certainties he once felt by instinct.

"I don't know! For something, some one thing, it's too late. There's something all behind me now, even the illusion of it, and I can't have it back, and you'll leave, you'll go away again, and I'll be all alone!" She falls silent, then he feels her begin to shiver. "Or I'll go."

"You're cold," he says after a moment. "Let's go back inside."

"No."

"Wait," he says, and he walks around the side of the house to peer into the kitchen window, where Harvey sits alone in the yellow light, his hands loosely wrapped around the glass. Daniel continues circling the house and spots Calvin in the study. Calvin bends to light a fire in the fireplace. Tomás has disappeared somewhere. Daniel hurries back to Ruby. "It's just Harv in the kitchen. Let's go in."

When they step in, Harvey looks up, eyes ill focused. Ruby glances around nervously as if the place were strange and dangerous. Harvey watches her, his whole body limp and sagging against his chair, as she glides around the room then alights on a chair across from him. She folds her hands in front of her on the table and studies her school ring.

"Have some whiskey," Harvey says, his tongue tangling in the syllables, bogging in the *m* and tripping with a whistle on the *k*. "Daniel?" He gestures toward the bottle. "Rube? Join me in a drink."

"No," Ruby says without looking up.

"Why the hell not?"

"I really don't drink anymore," she answers wearily.

"Bullshit! Since when?"

Ruby shrugs, knots her fingers in a new way. "I don't go for any of that stuff anymore." She pulls a tissue from her pocket and dabs at the mascara around her eyes.

Harvey stares at her, but from convenience, not concentration, to rest his eyes. Then he leans back to look at Daniel, who remains standing behind Ruby. "Come on, Daniel, for old times."

Ruby becomes very still, perhaps holding her breath. Daniel senses she wants him to say no and for that reason he considers having a shot with Harvey, but he thinks it a poor time to lose command of his senses. "Naw. Not now." Ruby's shoulders settle.

"Whiskey's the stuff. Good ol' Jack. Black Label. The best, fuckin'-A right!" Harvey sips with considerably less enthusiasm than his words imply. His face is swollen, waterlogged. Even his lips glisten overmoist. "Eases the pain."

"You're making it worse," Ruby says to her hands.

"I am?! You think I am?" he shouts. "Think again, think again. You've already convicted Dad, like that makes anything better. You can't blame it all on him. It's not his fault Mom—"

"No, 'it's not his fault Mom!' But it is his fault *me*! And her fault too. Don't you even know, Harvey?" she yells. "Goddamn it! Quit pretending. Quit looking the other way. Dad—your dad, not mine—raped me! Can I make it any plainer? Why haven't you ever believed me?" Ruby's eyes click to Daniel as if to measure the damage of this final revelation, so long unsaid though it inhabited their every previous moment together. She turns away from both of them.

"That's bullshit!" Harvey rages back at her.

"No, it isn't! And you know it. Why haven't you ever—"

"Aaaawww!" Harvey's inarticulate yell drops off to a grunt, then a moan. "Awww, hell. What was I supposed to do about it? I didn't really know. I thought there was something weird. You never said, not exactly. I never knew where all this weird shit begins and ends—you, Dad, Mom."

Daniel can't sit still any longer. "Ruby, why didn't you ever tell me? Maybe I could have done something."

"Like what? What would you have done? And look what it makes me. You were the last person I wanted knowing. You were the last guy who ever saw innocence in me. Somehow when people, when guys, know about this kind of thing, they mark you as easy. Like a sex toy. Oh, God, it all makes me sick. And it's all so creepy that everybody—my mom, my real dad, all you guys—kept looking away, ignoring the truth, or denying it, anyway. And that made it seem all right, like the world thought it was all right, and it's fucked me up but good!"

They all sit silent a moment. Harvey's face has gone vague and blubbery.

"I can take care of myself now," Ruby hisses through her teeth, her features clear and sharply etched. "But she sacrificed me. She encouraged me, in some weird way. You can be guilty for what you don't do, you know—not only for what you do."

Harvey looks down in a gesture of submission.

"I'm sorry, Harv," she says. "Look, it's not your fault. But don't go along with the lies anymore. I'm trying to spread the hurt around. God knows there's enough for everybody. I'm sorry. I love you." She reaches across the table to touch his hand. "I remember when you were born, when they brought you home. I was three and a half. Mom was . . . it was like she was in a spotlight, all glowing: my little brother. She never gave me a reason to feel jealous, either. I don't know how she did it. Somehow she shared you with me, brought me into that circle. She could be a good mother."

"Yeah." Harvey sighs. "It's all right." His hand lies quiet beneath his big sister's. "I'm not mad at you. It's easier to act that way."

"Don't get all plastered tonight," she urges, her fingers stroking across his knuckles.

"Too late." His eyes lurch to Daniel, and he smiles. "I don't feel so good."

"Are you going to be sick?" she asks, all sisterly concern.

"In a minute. What are you going to do, hold my forehead?"

Now she looks at him without answering. Harvey stands up slowly, ambles past Daniel, dragging his boot heels across the linoleum floor, and steers himself down the hallway toward the bathroom. In a moment, Daniel and Ruby hear the unmistakable coughing bark, followed by another, then the rattle of water in the pipes from the toilet flushing.

"Mom didn't understand men," Ruby says as though continuing an interrupted train of thought, as though this were a subject that had no connection to her life. "I don't think she liked them at all. She doesn't have any brothers. Then when Harvey was born, I think she was scared or, not scared, but . . . uneasy. I think she really wanted another girl, and it would be the three of us standing against all of you. Poor Harvey. She didn't know what to do with him. Sometimes I think she only had so much love to give. She gave him what she could, I guess. Like with Dad, it was her way."

"I always thought she liked me," Daniel says, because this time it seems safer to talk than to let Ruby loose in monologue.

"Oh, she did, and Lester. I know it doesn't make any sense. We used to talk about you, about what Daniel was doing, maybe what you would become, what kind of man, or what you'd do in college. But you know, as you got older, she got a little leery of you, because of me, because I was getting older too, and she didn't want me confiding in someone else, she didn't want those quiet, gentle moments going to someone else, even you. And I suppose she didn't want you to know too much—so much of her was wrapped up in me."

Ruby's face is smooth marble, a slight sheen to her skin as she sits rigid, staring into the past. The rest of the house is quiet and Daniel hears the wall clock's subtle grinding as the second hand sweeps across the numbers: it is nine thirty-seven, and then it is not anymore.

"Should I go check on Harvey?" he asks from a habit of assuming her permission is required for the unfolding of all action around her, each moment flowering from her into the present. She hasn't moved, not even her eyes flicker to acknowledge his question. In this strange limbo he watches her frozen face and all the sounds of the house magnify in his ears, the clock grinding, the refrigerator fan humming low, his breath now whistling through his nose. "Ruby," he says more forcefully.

At last she looks up.

"I wonder if maybe you should check on him, you know?" he says.

Her eyes rove his face, from one eye to the other to his mouth as he speaks, trying to read his new tone.

"Oh," she says, her eyes wrinkling in a familiar reflex of coy mischief. "I was just . . . I'll go." She stands in one fluid motion, still capable of filling his awareness. She sets her hand on the doorjamb and glides from the room. He can see how she forgets him in the small distracted movement of her fingers brushing a lock of hair behind her ears while bobbing her head, a movement of pure self-possession. Queen of this moment, she instructs him in reigning over his own universe. He sits in banishment, outside the charmed circle for the first time, outside with the wolves, nothing left for him to do but weigh the consequences of choice.

He hears nothing at first, she walks so silently. The clock, the refrigerator, the whistling in his nose return upon him. He reaches for Harvey's bottle, unscrews the top, and sniffs, letting the prickly warm whiskey vapors fill his nose all the way to his eyes. Then Harvey's staccato rumbling voice reaches his ears, followed by the higher melodic lilt of Ruby. He can't distinguish their words, but Ruby's tone is soothing and Harvey's replies smooth themselves, lose their serrated edge. In a few minutes the talking stops. The click of a door handle flashes bright, followed by more silence.

Then Ruby: "Dad?" The word sharply resonant in her throat, no trace of her customary flirty lilt.

He grows impatient to be done with this day, but he can't quite let it go yet, so he heads down the hallway toward the study and the bedrooms. He notices the bathroom light is off. A strip of light under Harvey's door brings him to a stop, and he stills his breathing to listen, at first to silence, then a murmured question from Harvey followed by Calvin. He speaks in the same quiet tones he uses to great effect on horses, when the melody is more important than the words. Daniel presses closer to the closed door. ". . . a reddish tint to it," Calvin was saying. "It was lighter when you were a baby, not so dark like it is now. So I told your mother you were my little gem, my little ruby: Ruby. When you were this big"—Daniel pictures him measuring a child's height from the floor to his hand—"I could make you smile just by saying that, 'my little Ruby.'"

Ruby murmurs so low Daniel can't hear. He pushes the door open and steps in. They all look at him and Ruby nods slightly, bringing him into their conversation. Calvin keeps talking. "And you know, it's funny. At first your mother didn't like that nickname. She thought it sounded cheap. She wanted you to be called by your full name, Maryanne, because it was her aunt's name. But then it got to growing on her too. That was about the time we decided we'd stay on the ranch for good. I sometimes think you made that decision for her, by being born here. That was when she started to love this place. She kinda hunkered down in. I never worried about losing her again after that. But I knew it wasn't me that was keeping her. And I've always thought," his voice wavers, suddenly faint and directionless, "I always thought, if she'll stay by me, I'll let her do whatever she wants to be happy. Just so she's here in the morning, sharing some little part."

"Daddy," Ruby says, her voice clear and strong. Daniel had come to back her up, but now he sees she doesn't need the help.

"It's that I'm going to miss her so much, and I feel like it's all my fault somehow."

"I'll never, ever come back into this house again," Ruby says. "I have the journals and they're going to tell everything and then everyone will know about you, about what you did, and you can't stop me. I know where she is, Daddy. I mean I have a pretty good idea, and I'm going up there. Why don't you tell me exactly, okay? Do me the right thing for once."

"I want you to pray with me, Ruby. It seems like we should," Calvin says. He bows his head and exhales heavily. "Dear God," he begins, but Ruby interrupts, "Dad—" and he says, "Shhh . . ."

"You can't hush me anymore," she answers, still with a decisive calm in her voice. "It's not only you and Mom. You have a responsibility to me too. I have a right to know what you've done. I want you to want me to know. I don't want any secrets anymore," she says.

Ruby's words hang alone for a moment. Then Harvey says, "Ruby's right, Dad. Let's get it all out."

"There are some things between man and wife that even a child can't know," Calvin answers. Daniel feels the silence expanding to fill the room, a pressurized swelling like pain inflating the atmosphere. Then Calvin again begins, "Dear God, we are thankful for Your forgiveness, and we trust in Your everlasting love to guide us."

"She's up above Water Canyon. It's obvious. Just tell me where," Ruby insists.

"Sometimes you are so much like your mother," Calvin says, giving up on the prayer. "There was so little compromise in her nature. But she always felt compromised. I suppose I had something to do with that. I've done some terrible things. But this was her last wish, and I obeyed. Yes, it's above Water Canyon. I'll go up with you. . . ."

"No, we'll go alone," Ruby interjects.

"Not me," Harvey breaks in. "Maybe later . . ."

After a while Calvin says, "Apocalypse is personal. I think that's what I've learned from . . . everything. That is the final lesson. And it's a process, not an event. When the seventh seal is broken, when the moon turns a bloody red and the stars fall from the sky and every mountain is removed from its place— all that takes time. We do it over a lifetime. I've never known what to make of Revelation. It's what kept me out of seminary. It's a terrible thing: the end of everything. That's pretty much where we're at, isn't it, as a family?"

26.

CALVIN SQUEEZES OUT OF THE ROOM past Daniel. Ruby looks up at him and says, "I want to talk to Harvey a little bit."

"Okay," Daniel says, suddenly overcome by wanting to get out of the McCullough house. He heads down the hall and through the front door. Outside he finds Tomás standing on the front porch smoking a cigarette. "I always liked her, Daniel," he says as if answering a question. "She didn't think so these last few years." Tomás rarely talks about emotions. "But I'm loyal to Calvin. He's loyal to me."

Daniel nods invisibly in the dark.

"She never wanted me to work out at Turkey Springs, on the archaeology. My ancestors were Indian, you know. *Genizaros* is the word for them. They settled in Los Ojos because they wanted to be Christians. The king of Spain granted them land. We have worked that land for two hundred years. But the other Indians hated us. Los Ojos was an outpost back in those days, the edge of civilization. To the west and north was the Apaches, the Navajos, the Utes. That's why there aren't any towns west, not old ones. We kept the light of Christianity, even when there weren't any priests. We did it ourselves, among ourselves, the brotherhood. We draw our strength from that commitment. Rae never understood that. Our roots here are in the church—that is why we're here. She didn't want me working on any dig. I told her, way back when she first discovered that old ruin, that I thought she shouldn't be messing with it, that it wasn't right, her digging around there."

"Why? It's science," Daniel contends.

"What science? Tell me what she learned. Tell me how digging up that old ruin is different from robbing graves at a cemetery down in Albuquerque."

"We learn something about ourselves from observing others," Daniel suggests. "From studying other cultures, maybe we can apply those things to our own lives, learn lessons from their past so we can live a better life. There's an evolution, some kind of progress through developmental stages. That's what I think."

"Bah! If she wanted to learn something, why didn't she come live in Los Ojos? I told her that once: come live in the village if you want to learn about an 'indigenous' culture. We've been here forever. We're real people, living and breathing, same as her. But she wanted to poke around for magic, like a *bruja*. I know something about *brujas*, witches, whatever. Sometimes you see them at night here." His cigarette gestures toward the fields in front of the house. "Little lights flickering along the edge of the trees. If you pull out your handkerchief and twirl it around three times like this"—the cigarette whirls in a circle—"and throw it on the ground, when you come back in the morning, the witch will be dead on the ground there. That's what they say, anyhow." A tone like irony rounds his voice.

"Do you believe that, Tomás?"

"Daniel, you and me, we've done a lot together, *qué no*? Lots of time together in the saddle. You make a pretty good horseman. You've got light hands on the bit, and I can tell how you watch your horse's ears to see what he's thinking. But you know, you can't ever really tell what he's thinking: maybe he wants to go back home and have a drink of water, or buck you off and go running across the vega like he was meant to run, nothing on his back. That's how most of life is, huh? Every time you climb on that horse's back, you take it for granted he's gonna do certain things, or else you'd never even get on. Now sometimes, he's a little loco, and he bucks and runs away with you, huh? Even if he dumps you in the sagebrush, you get back on, because you believe he'll be okay this time. But you never really know. That's how it is in the everyday world. Is it gonna snow tomorrow? Maybe. Am I gonna die tomorrow? Maybe.

"So tell me, what do you mean 'believe'? What do you really believe? What do you know, no bullshit, no 'maybe'? I'm not real educated, like you and like Rae was. Shit, I dropped outa school when I was thirteen. But I know what I know, and I know what I believe, and I don't have to hunt for it on my hands and knees with a trowel digging through some old Indian's garbage. 'Maybe this was where they kept their corn in the winter. Maybe this is where the old men prayed, but not the women. Maybe they moved away because the water dried up.' You know what I'm saying. Don't take me the wrong way. You're my friend. It's a question of faith. I'm not saying mine's any better than anybody else's. It's just mine, that's all. My ghost won't be out roaming these fields at night, looking for a place to rest. I'll be home." He flicks the cigarette butt and it flies end over end into the night to land sparking and bouncing on the driveway.

"You think Ruby's the same?" Daniel asks.

"No! Ruby doesn't live with 'maybe.' She's different that

way. But quit thinking about her. That's my advice to you. It's you I'm asking. You. What do you really believe in?"

Tomás and Daniel stand together in silence, both cold with their hands in their pockets, Daniel listening for sounds from the house.

"Then why did you help Calvin?"

"What?" Tomás responds.

"Why did you help Calvin take her body out there instead of giving her a real Christian burial. Why did you help him fake it?"

"Who says we faked it?"

"C'mon, Tomás. I know what's going on. Isn't it blasphemy or something? It's crazy," Daniel insists.

"I never said I wasn't crazy, Daniel." Tomás turns toward him and Daniel can smell sweet, strong liquor on the older man's breath. "Rae wanted it that way. What should I have done? It's not a bad thing, it's not wrong, God doesn't care. We prayed for her, we sang. It's a holy place."

"It seems hypocritical, that's all. It doesn't bother me. I'm trying to understand it."

Tomás laughs. "You can't understand everything, Danny. Don't think so much. Sometimes you have to stand in a place and watch it all happen. Then sometimes you don't."

"I do. I am," Daniel agrees. "Maybe it's time to do something else."

"We've been watching these people a long time, *qué no*?" Tomás asks.

"No lie," Daniel agrees. "So why do we do it?"

He can feel Tomás shrug in the dark. "I don't have anyplace else to go. And like I said, they're like family. I love Ruby, and I loved Rae, once. I guess you know by now—it doesn't matter—Ruby is my daughter. I thought by staying close by,

I could keep an eye on her, you know? Watch her grow up, help out somehow." He quickly adds: "But maybe you do have someplace else to go, huh? A life to get on with?"

"Maybe I'll stay," Daniel counters. "For good, this time."

"Even without Ruby?" Tomás presses him.

"Maybe," Daniel says. "Why?"

"She won't stay here," Tomás argues. "She'll go where she can be someone else."

27.

TOMÁS GOES INSIDE, and Daniel pauses with his hand on the door because he hears a car rolling along the road, then lights appear and it is Lester's old Dodge headed off toward the bunkhouse. He watches the car go by, its brake lights flashing red, then the lights go off and the engine quits and the night is silent again. Daniel waits to hear the door slam shut, but Lester apparently has not left the car. Daniel steps back into the warm house.

Ruby comes to him as if she has been waiting. "That was the fucking weirdest conversation of my life," she says. "Let's go. I just want to go to sleep," she says, brushing hair back from her face.

"Do you want to stay in here? In your old room? I'd understand."

"No. Oh, no."

"Lester came back. His car is over at the bunkhouse. I think he's waiting for us."

"Oh. I can't deal with him, Daniel. I can't. It's too weird." She shakes her head.

"Want me to go talk to him?"

"Please?" Her voice is so small that he reaches out to touch her, but her body is stiff and unyielding.

"Okay," he says, withdrawing his hand.

"Come back and get me," she says.

He finds Lester in the car, as he had expected, sitting upright with his hands on the wheel, staring out through the windshield as if he were driving a particularly straight stretch of road. Daniel stops beside the car and Lester turns to look at him: he has shaved his head and beard, and the shiny skin glistens in the light from the bunkhouse porch. Daniel steps back so Lester can open the door and get out.

"Hey," Daniel says in greeting.

"Hey." Lester runs his hands over his bald head. "I'm freezing. Let's go in."

Inside his room, Daniel turns on the light, then the heater, while Lester sits down.

"You shaved," Daniel says, and they both laugh.

"Yeah. I felt old today. Mortal. I've been reading Rae's journals. She once told me I should, you know, someday. There are these whole sides to her I didn't know, and I always thought I knew her, like better than I knew anybody else. She gave me this new way to see myself. I was important to her. I only read the last few years. She wrote a lot, sometimes about the weather, a lot about the dig, about her family, God, Indians, horses. About Calvin and Ruby. It's all there, like Ruby said."

Daniel has never seen Lester without his beard, and now he does seem, in fact, like a different person. "Is that why you shaved everything?"

"How do you mean?"

"Seeing yourself a new way?"

"Yeah, I guess so." Lester rubs his head again. "It feels pretty far out. I was born totally bald, and my mom used to say they wondered if I'd ever have any hair. I haven't cut it for ten years or so, and now I shave it off clean as a cue ball. Pretty wild . . ."

"I kinda like it."

"Ha! It's a sign of mourning. You're not supposed to like it. Rae once told me that's what the Apaches do when somebody close to them dies. Their hair is a sign of power, I guess. When that person goes, the remaining people lose a little of their power. Tomás is probably part Apache, you know. That means Ruby is too. Maybe that's the thing about her that Rae could never accept." He pauses a moment, his eyes going far off. "I'm going to move away from here. I decided. Want the house up in the village? The Navajos even abandon their hogans when a relative dies. I thought maybe if you were coming back up here, if Ruby . . ."

"I don't think so," Daniel begins. "I don't know what's going on. This is all new territory for everybody. It's like we're all temporarily insane. Grief is an altered state of consciousness, I'm convinced. Calvin, Ruby, you, everybody is all intensely themselves is what I keep thinking. It's like we're all exaggerating ourselves, but everyone's all pulled back in at the same time, pulled in so deep. It's like a movie. There's this sense of watching everything happen around you."

Whether Lester agrees or not, he nods, his eyes motionless staring into a shadowed corner of the room.

"Don't move away, Les. Stick around a while, think about it. It seems like the wrong time to be making a big decision."

"I've been thinking about it a while. I've been here for years. I stay much longer and it'll be the rest of my life. What's happened to me here at the ranch has happened, and it won't happen again, and if I stay I'll always be looking back." He falls silent.

"I understand, actually," Daniel says. "But I've got to stay close—to Ruby, to this place right now. I went away once before, and I almost blew it. Not again. I feel like it's time to see it through to the end."

"Well," Lester says, "it might not be what you want, but it might be what you need."

They sit still and let a bit of quiet pass between them, sometimes catching each other's eyes and looking away not hurriedly but from courtesy, a respect for the privacy of the other's thoughts. It is a way of being together that they have developed during all the dawn-to-dusk days working on the ranch, stringing fence and shoeing horses and inoculating cattle.

"Where are you going to go?" Daniel asks finally.

Lester rouses himself to answer. "I'm thinking Africa. Yeah. It's something Rae and I used to talk about doing. Always off in the future, somewhere down the road, when—when what? I wonder. That's what I keep thinking, what were we waiting for? But I've got some money saved and all." He rubs the top of his head again. "She didn't kill herself, Daniel. I know it for a fact. The journals would say something, though I still can't figure why on earth she kept them stashed underground. There was something ritualistic about that, something about it being a sacred space. Anyhow. She was happy. Pretty happy. As happy as she ever was. I don't think she was going crazy, either, she was just—different. Learning. Calvin's wrong on this one."

"Where are they, the diaries?"

"I've got 'em in the car. I wanted to drop them by before I leave. And the will is there too. I don't know how legal it is, but it does have a witness signature. Ruby should have them, at least. Is she coming over here tonight? I wanted to say good-bye."

"How about tomorrow? She's exhausted."

"I'm leaving now," Lester says.

"Now?"

"Yeah. The car's all packed. You can have everything else in the house up in the village. I've got a letter for Calvin in the car, and one for Harvey. And I talked to Tomás after dinner. That's everybody, now I've seen you. I left a letter for you at my house. First I'm gonna walk up and look at this burial rack Calvin built."

"You know where?"

"It's pretty obvious when you read the journals."

"Above Water Canyon, out on the western point," Daniel guesses.

"That's where she'd go to talk with the coyotes." Lester stands. "Ruby'll know the spot. It's way up high." He stands. "Let me give you those diaries."

They go back outside. "You sure you can make it up there?" Daniel asks. "There's no moon."

"I'll find it." They both look up at the sky, opaque with clouds. "Smells like snow," Lester comments. He leans into the backseat, which along with Rae's strongbox is piled with miscellaneous accumulated objects of Lester's simple life: a guitar, an older desk lamp, a down parka, an art print Rae had once given him, a rifle. He hefts the strongbox off the seat. "Here." Now he goes to the front and pulls out two envelopes. "One for Calvin, one for Harvey. I really thought I'd see Ruby tonight. If you want to be with her, you've got to tell her so. There's nothing comes of waiting. Nothing comes of nothing."

They regard each other a moment, then Daniel sets the box down by the bunkhouse door. "Africa," he says. "Won't you need a passport, shots, Great White Hunter license?"

Lester waves the question away, saying, "Details, details. I'm goin'."

"Hippie Cowboy Great White Hunter."

"You got it."

"With a clean head."

"I'm lettin' it grow out," Lester answers and they both laugh. "Later, man." He reaches his hand out and Daniel realizes they have only shaken hands once before, the day Lester arrived at the ranch.

Lester climbs into the car and starts the engine after several cranks of the starter. "I'm gonna park up at the pond, hike it from there. I don't want to wake you when I leave. I'll see you." The car lurches backward with a spurt of gravel and Daniel turns away.

After setting the strongbox with the journals under the bed, Daniel heads for the house with the letters for Calvin and Harvey. He finds Ruby walking toward him.

"All right?" he asks.

"Yes."

"Lester's moving away tonight."

"What else could he do?"

"He wanted to see you before he left."

Ruby shakes her head. "What is there to say? I know Mom was in love with him. He was my friend too. But Dad is in there"—she nods toward the study—"and it all hurts too much."

"He left me a letter to give your dad, and one for Harv. I need to take them up to the house. I'm going to miss him."

Ruby leans into him and her garden scent is all around him, filling him with an overwhelming nostalgia.

"I know exactly where she is, the corpse," Ruby says. "You'll go with me tomorrow?"

"Of course."

"Do you understand why I don't want to say good-bye to Lester?"

"I guess so."

"When he came here was when everything started to happen, the really heavy stuff." She steps apart from Daniel, dropping his hand to comb her hair back with her fingers and zip her jacket tighter around her throat. "He reminds me of things, things that are hard to think about right now." She pushes against him for balance and stands. "Why don't you take those letters up to Dad."

"I talked to Mom for a long time, that night after the Fourth of July barbecue," Ruby tells him as they walk in the dark back to the bunkhouse after Daniel has dropped Lester's letters on the kitchen table in the main residence. "It was the first time we really talked woman to woman, not mother to child. I didn't know it would be the last time I ever saw my mother. We talked about Lester. She said, if she were really a Christian, she would consider him a saint. I told her he didn't seem very saintly to me, he did drugs, he drank, he swore, he committed adultery. She said it didn't have anything to do with any of that: 'He is completely true to himself.' Let's take a walk around the field before we go in. Maybe we'll see some deer."

"Okay."

"The moon won't rise tonight till very late, maybe three in the morning," she says. "It's so dark with these clouds. —It made her cry. Do you know I don't remember ever seeing her cry before? She said she could never live up to Lester's expectations. I didn't realize it then, but what bothered her most was his forgiveness: being the way he was, he forgave her every day. He would stand by her forever, even knowing everything. About Dad and me, about Tomás. I think she really wanted to get a divorce last summer. It's not that Lester was putting any pressure on her. I don't think he cared about that, the legal part. I doubt they ever thought of getting married. But now, even just seeing Lester around . . . I don't blame him for anything, I'm not even angry with him anymore. But he symbolizes the complete breakdown of my family, somehow."

They have reached the point where the road curves around the southern end of the hay fields. In the quiet they can hear the small, ripping sound of deer eating, their teeth tearing away the alfalfa stalks left from the last cutting of the season. "They're so tame, they don't even run away from us," Daniel says.

"When I was a little girl, I thought everybody must have deer in their front yard. We belong here, they belong here, they don't mind. We don't kill them. I couldn't believe it once, when I was maybe twelve, Daddy took Harvey hunting up in the mountains and they came riding back in with this beautiful buck thrown over Hatchet's back. I cried and cried. That was when I knew men were different. Mom fought against men telling her who she was. She was afraid she'd become what they saw in her. I think that's why she got so contrary. But that night last July, she said I was foolish for turning away from you."

"Is that what you were doing, turning away? It felt like it."

"Well—look at how she was, paralyzed between two men. Three, with Tomás still around. I want to make sure I'm doing this for me. Is that selfish?"

"No, it's sensible," he answers.

"Sometimes I get the feeling that you need me to be something," she says. "It's like a pressure, a weight. I've never really been sure what you thought about me, I guess."

"That's because it seems like every time we've been together in the last year, like last Fourth of July, I was tongue-tied. I don't mean I was embarrassed or afraid to say something.

You somehow took away the whole basis for conversation. It didn't seem to make much sense to declare my love to you with David around."

"But you kept coming around," she says.

"Maybe it was more comfortable wanting you than having you. I thought you always set the terms between us, you know? It meant I never had to lay myself on the line. But that isn't fair to you, blaming you for all the false starts between us. I was afraid: if all I wanted was sex, this Puritan part of me says that's bad. So there's some safe place between wanting and having. I got addicted to the craving."

"I'm so sick of being a projection of men's lust." Ruby sighs. "David didn't do that to me. He gave me breathing room." Her voice sounds sad and tired. "He served his purpose. I always knew what you'd want from me in bed. He didn't ask for that. He's like a monk. He was safe. But you could have said something, anything, and I'd have dropped him in a heartbeat."

"But you didn't want me to do that, Ruby."

"You're right. I sort of did, but no, I didn't, not at all. No," she agrees.

"What about now?" he asks.

"What *about* now?" she returns.

"I'm here," he answers, as her hand, birdlike, flutters against his arm as if testing its reality or asserting her own presence in this world where she has materialized in the night. Daniel thinks of witches, handkerchiefs, the fluttering presence at his side.

28.

SPOONED AGAINST HIM IN THE BED, Ruby is the night, velvet and transformational, a planet orbiting a secret sun: for a few moments of almost playful flirting, she is the sleek embodiment of desire, infinite legs, a gliding smooth disintegration, the blackness with stars, impossible points of light that insist on utter emptiness between, as he imagines for the last time, she might insist: empty yourself here, leave yourself behind. But she doesn't. She is closed to him. Lying still, there now, quiet—shhh!—the world sleeps, dreaming its private secrets—mourning—she begins to cry, her eyelids squeezed shut, her breath a jagged stuttering.

"Ruby," he whispers, an invocation in the lightless night. Again desire has pulled him so far forward he seems to have overtaken himself and long since passed the reality of this girl he once thought he knew. The room is cold and the darkness hovers close with predatory patience. His fingers reveal tears on her cheek. He brushes them away, but she does not stop crying. Her hair is lush and hopeful as a child's prayer slipping through his fingers, slipping into empty air, everything slipping away from his grip. "I wish I could say something."

She shakes her head quickly, as if it hurts to move—he can

feel it—and so he lets her cry into the night, sharp sobs like a wall collapsing, time itself caving in, the very walls tumbling, a brick at a time, each memory, falling one by one past, a girl's world blown apart in darkness.

Or unfolding.

"Everything is ending," she says.

Even as he holds her he dozes and begins to dream cinematically: with Ruby and Harvey he is at the Turkey Springs ruin digging his fingers into the coarse sand around a giant slab of sandstone that lies flat on the ground. He lifts it. Behind him, Ruby is saying, "She has to be in there. I know it. I can feel it." But when he pulls the stone away, it reveals no burial chamber, only bare ground. Then Calvin speaks. "You're thinking of Jesus and the Resurrection, you know, the stone moved aside and all that. It could only happen once, to the Son of God. There aren't any miracles for us. The days of miracle are past."

Ruby shouts, "No! You're lying to us again. Look!" She points and they follow the command of her long finger: rippling blue water laps the rim of the hole. To Daniel she says, "You could have come with me."

"Daniel?" she says in a breathy whisper, loud enough to wake him.

"What?"

"When I die, don't bury me. It's too awful. I want to be cremated. Spread my ashes above Water Canyon. It has to be a very clear day, and windy, so they'll blow."

"Okay." Then in a moment, "Can you sleep?"

"Uh-huh."

"Are you comfortable? Want me to move to the top bunk?" he asks. The old mattress sags so deeply they must lie intertwined.

"No!" she whispers, nestling closer and sighing with the modulation of one resigned to a long siege of pain. "I want you to be here, when I die. When my life ends. Whenever that is"—her voice stretched like piano wires—"holding me like this."

29.

DANIEL NEXT AWAKENS TO A MUFFLED GRAY LIGHT emanating equally from earth and sky. He guesses it has snowed. With some disbelief he finds Ruby still nestled against him like a dream relic somehow hauled into daylight, her reality confirmed by the slow sleeping breaths she takes through her mouth, the way her hands reach out from a dream of her own to hold him as he slides quietly from under the musty blankets. She murmurs but her eyes stay shut fast and she adjusts easily to his absence, rolling into the warm place he has abandoned.

The room is cold, the linoleum icy to his bare feet, so he stoops to twist the dial of the gas heater before going to the window and moving aside the window drape to see the snow, an inch or two, so wet it sags the arms of a cholla cactus that stands above the arroyo behind the bunkhouse. Farther east, high beyond the oaks and cottonwoods and tamarisk that rise from the streambed, the cliffs of Mesa Reina stand solid against misty wet clouds. Small birds flit with apparent annoyance among the trees; they light on the very tips of cactus branches, they gather beneath an old piñon tree where the ground is bare.

Turning from the window, he sits in a chair by the heater with his feet on the bed and studies her sleeping form. She is almost unrecognizable, her face fleshy, the high cheekbones muted, the eyelids puffy. She looks childlike, unformed and unburdened by the betrayals and disappointments of life— unmarked, too, by the strangeness of her peculiar wisdom. He sees nothing that might ratify his captivation, and yet it remains.

Restless, he stands and stretches against the stiffness in his back, his legs. The vestigial gauze of dreaming still hangs about his awareness, the sensation of blurry figures slipping into the gray shadows of his peripheral vision, actors from dreams he cannot recall—but if he turned quickly enough, he might catch them in surprise, illuminate their secret ways, as Ruby sleeps, herself blurred and insubstantial in daylight. He goes again to the window, but its bleak scene turns him away: the world out there seems reduced by a dimension, the axis admitting humans having shrunk to zero. Is this like death, he wonders, when that long line of our life has retracted back into the center, back to zero, and there's no more room for us in this world? While Ruby sleeps, dreaming, Daniel waits for the next uncoiling of his life's line beyond these four walls, beyond her, the ending having stopped but the beginning not yet started.

Ruby stirs, groaning as she stretches out her arms and legs. "Ummmnnh!" She smiles at Daniel.

"Snow day," he announces, as if school were canceled and they could stay home and play all day.

"Good." She rolls onto her side. "You're all dressed and everything. Where you going?"

"Going crazy," he answers.

"Hmm." Her brown eyes are soft and round as she

considers him. "I like this, waking up and seeing you. It seems so natural."

"It could be," Daniel affirms.

"When I first woke up, I didn't remember, I mean about Mom, or Dad, or my life so far. I saw you sitting there and everything was perfect, like this was our honeymoon, our marriage—and it was all complete," while Daniel sees that nothing he might ever say or do will ease her pain, and it will always be with them, between them, infusing their bond whatever may become of them, together or apart. He must decide.

"Would you love me if I wasn't half crazy?" Ruby asks.

"No," he admits. "But if I wasn't half crazy too, I wouldn't be here in the first place."

She sits up, considering his words, keeping the blankets around her. "Maybe we can try again. Hand me my sweats?" He finds the clothes buried under his jacket on the bureau and gives them to her. "Have you been outside yet?" she asks as she dresses.

"I was waiting."

"Can we take the horses up through the snow?" she asks.

"I think so. It's just a dusting, really, but it's real wet."

Ruby stands up and goes to the mirror, combing her fingers through her hair and rubbing her eyes. "Ooh, look. Is that me? I look like the Bride of Frankenstein." Her hair is tangled, her mascara smeared around her eyelids. "Ever look in the mirror and it's like you're seeing yourself for the first time? Who is that person?" She nods at the glass. "I feel like I've stepped through, like Alice in Wonderland. I'm really afraid to go up there, Daniel. These waves come over me, my mind goes blank, and every thought I ever had gets washed away. I feel like a leaf, or a seed. A seed blowing around in the wind. I need you to stay with me, stay close, just a little longer."

First they stop by the house, where they find Calvin eating breakfast alone, digging through a bowl of oatmeal. "Harvey's still sleeping," he tells them.

"Sleeping it off," Ruby says.

"I guess so."

"I can't eat," Ruby tells Daniel. She turns to her father. "We have the will and all of Mom's journals."

He nods, looking down at his oatmeal. "That's what Lester said, in his letter. Someday I might read them. Or I won't. I guess everything is up to you now." He looks up to Ruby, over at Daniel, then back to Ruby again. "Are you moving back home, honey?"

"No, Daddy. No. Someday I know I'll have to forgive you. I'll come back and we'll make peace. But I have to forgive myself first, and then Mom. You're a ways down the line."

Calvin finishes eating, watching her talk, and Daniel senses that some part of Calvin has frozen into a block of ice, the habit of denial solidifying and numbing his responses to her. Calvin gets up and rinses his bowl in the sink, while Daniel pours himself coffee and Ruby gets juice from the refrigerator. Calvin carefully sets his bowl onto the wooden dish drainer, then turns to his daughter. "Don't go up there."

"Daddy, it's not up to you."

Calvin looks at Daniel. "It was Rae's wish, you know. She told me several times. It's in her will, though it's probably not legal. She couldn't stand the thought of being buried in the ground. I had to honor her wish. Daniel, can you understand that?"

Daniel finds Ruby's eyes upon him. "I would have done the same thing," Daniel says truthfully.

"Well." Calvin grabs his hat from where it sits upside down on its crown and walks through the pantry to the back door. "I've got animals to feed."

30.

AFTER LUNCH AND WAITING IN VAIN for the clouds to lift, Daniel and Ruby ride the arroyo trail, Ruby leading on Boca, and occasionally they stop to pick out snow from their horses' hooves, where it packs in hard snowballs in the hollow of their soles. Low, fast-moving clouds brush across the mesas from the north, and the snow falls in clumps from the trees and shrubs around them. The gusty wind has a wintry smell.

The trail follows the stream into Water Canyon, where floods in the summertime run blood red when a thunderstorm opens the sky, dropping a deluge of huge raindrops and hail onto the ranch and the mesas above, a torrent of water tinted by the red cliffs and the red walls of the canyon, which narrows to an overhung, almost cavernous box, the runoff cascading for an hour after the rain has ceased, draining all the land above it. Daniel has seen the water run six or eight feet deep, pushing boulders ahead of it, damming up against a downed tree and roaring like the sea. Afterward he has walked the stream, reduced to its normal trickle, and seen scarred bark on the cottonwoods as high as he could reach with his hand.

Daniel urges his horse into a trot to catch up. "Ruby?"

They stop, side by side, the wind blowing loose ends of Ruby's hair across her eyes. She's got a pack with the journals slung over her saddle horn. "After this, what?" he asks.

"After which?" She looks confused.

"What will you do after you see . . . ?" He presses, hoping one last time to find a clue to his own destiny in her actions, one last time to find himself beyond that pulsing emptiness finally confirmed yesterday by the river. "It's only a body, you know," he tells her now. "A dead body."

Her brow relaxes its quizzical furrowing. "I don't know, Daniel. What? I want you to tell me what's next. All this other stuff: Mom, Dad, Lester—it's over." The sun now breaks through, then goes away again so the world glints an instant before going dull. "I'll be free," she says, then: "Or I never will." The wind picks up and she holds her hair back with one hand and smiles. "I have this Beatles song in my head, one line. Isn't that silly? 'What do you see when you turn out the lights?' Well, I know it's mine." She laughs. "It's so dumb, I know. I should be solemn. I'm not really that deep, you know. What do you see when you turn out the lights, Daniel?"

It used to be I could only see you, he thinks, but instead he says, "Nothing. The dark."

"It's a matter of where you look, don't you think?" she says. "That's what Mom taught me to do, go ahead and explore it. We're living in the dark, but if you know where to look—"

"You can talk to angels," he interrupts, anticipating her thoughts.

"Now you're making fun of me."

"No, Ruby."

"It doesn't matter, as long as they listen!" She is joking, but her smile caves in as she takes her bottom lip in her teeth. "After this, Daniel? What if there is no 'after'? What if this goes on forever and ever?" She waves her hand distractedly at the canyon walls, the trees, the sky. "This is it."

On the mesa top high above the canyon two hours later, the horses carry their heads low and their ears back, walking slowly into the wind that blows hard and steady from the northwest. Here the cliffs run westward to a peak shaped like the bow of a ship plowing toward sunset. They ride parallel to the rim but back from it in the trees, a stunted forest of piñon and juniper where the snow lies several inches deep. Hidden rocks continually trip the horses. They stumble and grunt with irritation. He lets Ruby pull ahead so he can feel free and alone, as if this were his ride, not hers. Occasionally the way emerges into brief clearings where Daniel can see ahead to the point of the mesa. Once he spots two poles jutting into the sky. Colored cloths wave like flags on a mast.

Ruby reins in her horse below a series of rock ledges almost like stairs leading to the top. Winding through the trees to the right is the faint impression of a road—nothing more than two deep ruts drifted over with snow—which must run north to Cañoncito. Ruby has dismounted when he reaches her and swings himself from the saddle. Turk rubs his head against him, itchy where the sweat has dried under his bridle. Daniel's face stings in the wind that drives a powdery snow off the tree branches and rock above them.

"Does this road go up to the top? I can't remember," he says.

"No, it just circles." She gestures with her hand, a vague twirling that suggests endless repetitions. "When we rode yesterday, I had no idea we were so close. I don't know why I didn't think of it. If we'd turned left instead of right . . ."

"I thought I saw something a few minutes ago," he says.

"I did too."

"Should we leave the horses down here and hike the last bit?" Daniel says.

"Yes. The easiest way is right along the rim. There's no brush and the snow's all blown away." Ruby approaches, slides her arms around him, and studies his face.

"We could go back," he says.

"No. But let me go ahead," she says, stepping away from him, her eyes bright and steady. "I want a little time alone."

He takes the reins from her. "Okay. But listen: the sun's gonna set soon. I don't want to ride the canyon in the dark."

"Go on back if you want," she says as if releasing him. "I can get myself home."

He nods. "All right. I was thinking the same thing."

Her hand floats to his face and she tiptoes to kiss him. "I love you. Come find me when you're ready." She turns away without letting him answer.

He leads the horses a hundred yards down the snowy road, finding a small hollow where trees break the strongest gusts. Talking to them softly and about nothing, he ties Turk and Boca by their halter ropes to thick, shoulder-high branches. They are tired from the ride and seem content to stand quietly while he loosens the saddle cinches and slips the bits from their mouths. After this ride, he thinks, he will pull Turk's shoes and turn him out to winter on the flats across the highway. Then next spring he will move the horse down closer to the city.

Daniel checks that the horses are not overheated from the climb, then he trudges back up the road, picking up Ruby's tracks where she had left him, following them to the edge of the mesa overlooking the ranch, the black line of the highway, the grassy pastures on either side of the river, then Animas Peak and the rest of the mountains to the south.

Her tracks turn west, up the rocky climb to the summit. Mostly the route is windswept clean. Sometimes the going pitches up so steep and the wind gusts so strong he must steady himself with his fingertips on the coarse rock, which is green with lichen and pocked by tiny puddles of melted snow like miniature ponds. He scrambles on, stopping after a few minutes to catch his breath and let Ruby extend her lead.

He sits down and dangles his feet over the cliff. Below him the earth falls away, first a hundred-foot drop to a sagebrush meadow, then another short plunge to yet another meadow, then the rounded, voluptuous rocks that cap the final cliffs above the home pasture. He thinks of Ruby ahead of him, climbing out of sight into the wind. He lets his eyes roam the huge landscape below until he grows cold deep inside and feels his legs stiffening, then he stands and stretches and moves on.

The sun slips out for a moment, slanting low and throwing a silvery light into his eyes. A dark shape flutters down toward him from the peak. Momentarily blinded, he instinctively ducks, thinking it's a red-tailed hawk accelerating with the west wind in a steep dive, but as it passes he sees it's a bandanna. It blows past the lip of the mesa and lifts up slightly, writhing and twisting alive before it catches in a downdraft, floating out of sight toward the meadow below. Daniel continues, reaching the top in a few minutes. The rack stands before him. He sees how Ruby's tracks have circled it, but the snow all around looks trampled and confused. She is nowhere in sight.

Bits of paper lie scattered on top of the snow and on the ground where it is bare and stuck wetly on the rock. Some of the pieces are burned. Daniel stoops to pick one up. He immediately recognizes Rae's unusual cursive handwriting. The ink is smeared and unreadable. Without trying to decipher it, he lets it fly into the wind.

Then he approaches the rack and grabs one of the vertical posts, which is sunk deeply into the ground and does not wiggle when he leans his entire weight against it. Several feet off the ground, a platform of pine and aspen stretches between the uprights. The whole thing is lashed tightly together with baling wire. Each pillar is decorated at the top with a bright scarf, except one.

Daniel hops onto a rock to look at the burial rack. The wind has kept off the snow and in the middle he sees only a long, familiar hank of hair—Lester's ponytail—draped across the open spine of a notebook, most of its pages torn out, the rest freshly charred black. Otherwise the platform is empty. Ruby must have tried burning the book to let all Rae's secrets die with her—it's her act of forgiveness, he thinks—but then given up because of the wind and instead she shredded the pages, finally replacing Lester's offering out of respect.

Now the sun flares orange, setting quietly in the wind, igniting the clouds in a rich, apocalyptic glow. A bit higher in the sky, Venus glimmers in and out of the clouds.

Cupping his hands to his mouth, Daniel yells, "Ruby!"

The wind snatches away her name.

Daniel walks along the edge of this jutting rock, looking for another way off, the path Ruby might have taken. The sides sheer away and the passages down through the rock are clogged with wiry scrub oak and twisted pine bent and contorted by years of steady wind. She must know her own way down. Perhaps she doubled back to the horses somehow when he was daydreaming on the cliff below.

He calls again, less forcefully, but again the wind muffles

his voice. Alone in the wilderness, with the sky surrounding and space beyond, the wind droning in the stiff limbs of ancient dwarfed pines, he sits down, the strength gone from his legs, as if the old notion of Ruby has at last become too heavy to bear. He needs a few minutes of rest to consider loving her now that desire is spent and truth told and no one else stands between them. It's up to him.